Aeris Legends 1:
The Huntsman and the Healer
A Prequel to Redeemer Chronicles

By Julie C. Gilbert

Aletheia Pyralis Publishers

http://www.juliecgilbert.com/
https://sites.google.com/view/juliecgilbert-writer/

Love Science Fiction or Mystery?
Choose your adventure!

Visit: http://www.juliecgilbert.com/

For details on getting free ebooks.

Dedication:

To my siblings: Thomas and Carrie.
Love you.

(There's no weird subtext in
dedicating this particular book to you.)

If you have not read *River's Edge Ransom*, you may wish to do so first.

If you wish to jump right in, check out the summary, What's Gone on
Before.

Maps available upon request, please email
Devyaschildren@gmail.com

Table of Contents:

Who's Who and What's What:

Aeris – a planet created by Kailon

People Types:
Saroth – A people who live on the east side of Aeris's main continent. They are usually Gifted in the darker four of the seven magic schools and tend to become Destroyers, Shapeshifters, Conjurers, or Minders.
Arkonai – A people who live mainly in the northwest corner of Aeris's main continent. They are usually Gifted in the lighter three of the seven magic schools and tend to become Seekers, Guardians, or Healers.
Bereft – Majority of people on Aeris who have no access to magic.

Key Saroth:
Marina Castaloni – former Destroyer, elder sister to Jackson and Gabriel
Jackson Castaloni – Conjurer, younger brother to Marina, older brother to Gabriel
Gabriel Castaloni – Shapeshifter (squirrel, wolf, beetle), younger brother to Jackson and Marina
Antonio Castaloni – Marina's father
Corabelle Castaloni – Marina's mother
Marcus Polani – betrothed to Marina in a marriage contract that exists between their houses
Kyle Ricci – Destroyer, Marina's friend

Key Arkonai:
Daniel Saveron – Seeker, Huntsman
Jordan Lekros – Guardian, Daniel's friend
Christa Arrington – Healer, Daniel's friend
Ashton Cassel – Arkonai Hunting Guild Supreme Huntmaster, Christa's uncle

Other:
Kailon – Eternal King, Creator of Aeris
The Lady – immortal servant of Kailon
Dark Man – Jackson's Master, a manifestation of the Outcast, an immortal who rebelled against Kailon

Key Locations: (maps available upon request)

Caramore – section of Aeris's main continent controlled by Saroth

Bastion – Arkonai capital city; seat of the High Council

Dominance – Saroth capital city; seat of the Tariku League

Aridel – Arkonai; located on the northwest side of Aeris's main continent

Temperance – neutral city; located in the center of Aeris's main continent

Outreach – neutral city; located on the southeast side of Aeris's main continent

River's Edge – Bereft village on the southwest side of Aeris's main continent; site of the controversy surrounding Marina

What's Gone on Before?

(Contains spoilers for *River's Edge Ransom*.)

In *River's Edge Ransom*, Jackson Castaloni lures his older sister, Marina, to the village of River's Edge by spreading a disease amongst the population. Then, in disguise, he hires a huntsman named Daniel Saveron to kill her.

Daniel captures Marina but discovers that she's been treating the sick villagers, not harming them. Unable to kill an innocent woman, Daniel breaks his contract and helps Marina tend to the villagers.

Marina's other younger brother, Gabriel, reluctantly draws her into a nearby forest where Jackson reveals himself and presents his deal. He admits to spreading Surdan's Bane amongst the villagers and offers Marina the cure in exchange for two things. One, she forfeits her Keeper's pendant, the magical object that would allow her passage home and a sign of her birthright as the firstborn. Two, her Destroyer Gifts.

Marina pays the ransom, but Jackson tries to kill her anyway after giving her a vial of the cure. Gabriel and Daniel defend Marina, and her brother receives a serious wound in the fight. Although Marina does not have her Destroyer Gifts, there's still magic within her. She uses some of her lifeforce and Daniel's strength to save her brother.

Prologue:
Watch and Wait

Combat Arena, Fort Medron

Jackson Castaloni finishes reading from the summoning scroll and watches in fascination as the prisoner before him changes.

As the dark spirit enters the man, he stiffens, screams, and thrashes against the chains holding him fast to the combat arena's stone walls. The struggle sends up a spray of sand as the man's feet kick furiously. He strains against the shackles, foams at the mouth, moans, and then goes strangely still, slumping against the wall. Sweat drips down his pale face.

Jackson takes an involuntary step backwards, surprised by the outburst. He has kept the man fed and watered, but the two days of captivity had taken their toll on the prisoner's spirit. Previously, the man's dark eyes bore a listless look. Now, they blaze with unholy, yellow light.

"I told you to break their spirits before the summoning ritual," scolds a raspy voice from the prisoner. It's definitely not the man's natural voice. This particular specimen—a condemned murderer—came from Dawtan Prison in Temperance. "Now, release me."

Swallowing his unease, Jackson does as bid. Pulling out a heavy key from an inner pocket in his robes, Jackson slips it into each wrist and ankle manacle before undoing the thick metal band that holds the man's waist to the wall.

"I apologize, Master," says Jackson. He humbly lowers his gaze and makes a courtly bow. "It won't happen again."

The figure straightens and examines the raw wrist wounds,

frowning.

"See that it does not," he mutters, "but no matter, this vessel shall suffice for now. It will last a few hours anyway. We will work on a more permanent solution later. There is much to discuss. Give me your report on the River's Edge affair."

Steeling his courage, Jackson clears his throat and squares his shoulders. He's not certain how the Dark Man will take the news he has to bear. Part of him suspects this is a test, for the physical extension of the Outcast must surely have many servants on Aeris. Briefly, Jackson considers holding certain details back, but one look into the figure's eyes cures him of that notion. He decides to break the worst news first.

"My sister is alive," Jackson admits.

"I know." The Dark Man's neutral tone conveys neither approval nor disapproval. The voice is stronger now, less wispy. "I had a feeling that might happen, but start the tale from the beginning."

"I followed your orders and brought Surdan's Bane down upon the village of River's Edge. It worked as you said it would, and as predicted, Marina took the bait. Eventually, I made the proposal and took her powers in exchange for the cure. She's probably still there ministering to those pathetic people."

"If she's without her Destroyer powers, why is she not dead?" inquires the Dark Man through the slave.

"Because the huntsman turned on us," says Jackson.

"Try again." The Dark Man's chuckle chills Jackson's soul. "What really happened?"

Two painful heartbeats pass before Jackson can answer the question.

"The huntsman ... and my brother turned on me." He lowers his gaze and dwells on the personal loss. A twinge in his shoulder reminds him of that terrible day. A few healing scrolls restored his burnt and bloody fingers and knit the flesh back together on his left shoulder, but he can still remember the pain well enough.

I'll have to deal with Gabriel eventually.

"That is unfortunate," consoles the Dark Man, "but give him time. Pursue peace with him for now. Gabriel may yet prove useful. You might have to show him how far you're willing to go to achieve your goals. You should also find a proper Conjuring master and develop your Gifts further. There's little more you can learn from the old fool you currently call master."

"Yes, Master." A surge of hope blossoms in Jackson's chest. He tries to quell it, but he can't. With Father and Marina devoted to the One and Mother openly undecided, Gabriel is Jackson's last hope for help and understanding from his family.

"I am surprised you tolerated a betrayal from him, but we can address that issue later," says the Dark Man. "Let us speak of your sister."

"I will kill her as promised," Jackson vows.

The figure holds up a hand to halt further assurances.

"No. Watch her carefully for now," orders the Dark Man. "See what she does."

"My lord?" Jackson's tone makes it a question.

"Marina's death at the huntsman's hands would have been good for turning your father against the Arkonai, but he is only one man. Alive, your sister may stir up more trouble than a hundred men." There's a thoughtful quality to the Dark Man's voice. He stares off into space for a short time before refocusing on Jackson. "As for your loyalty kill, the target must change. Who will it be?"

Jackson hesitates. Marina had been the easy choice. As his elder sister, she lay ahead of him according to Saroth tradition. Gabriel or Mother would be the next logical choice since they lie behind him in the succession, but Jackson cannot fathom ever killing them. It makes very little sense to kill Father while Marina yet lives.

"Your mother or your father?" prompts the Dark Man.

"Father," Jackson answers instantly, "but wouldn't that let Marina inherit—"

The Dark Man cuts him off with a sharp look.

"She has little use for the Castaloni lands and fortune," he says. Restless, he paces a small section of the combat arena, deep in thought. "And you can kill her after she's made a fine nuisance of herself."

"How would it be done?" Even Jackson doesn't know which kill he's really referring to. Marina won't be easy to get to as long as that huntsman stays with her. Father too has people watching over him.

"There are so many options." The Dark Man smiles. "Part of the fun is finding a fitting end for someone. For a man like your father, I believe poison will do best, a slow one that mimics a lingering disease."

He lapses into silence and paces for a solid minute before facing Jackson again.

"I shall have another servant deliver the poison when I decide on the right one. For now, keep a close eye on your sister."

"What do you hope she'll do?" asks Jackson.

"She has many dangerous ideas about uniting the Arkonai and the Saroth," says the Dark Man. "That will gather her many enemies and stir up strong feelings on both sides. If we work carefully, we can use her ideals to bring about further divisions."

"That would start a war," Jackson notes.

"War is a cleansing thing, my young servant. If you are to truly serve me, you must understand this. But we must be cautious not to let your sister succeed in her efforts to reconcile the differences between the magic races."

"Why do you say that?"

"Because peace is dangerous. It makes people weak," replies the Dark Man. "We want conflict and chaos." He gestures wildly to emphasize his point.

"Could I not accomplish that by dispensing with subtlety and claiming responsibility for the destruction in River's Edge?" Jackson wonders.

Letting his arms drop to his sides, the Dark Man conjures a thin dagger and studies it.

"You could, but that would get you killed, and you are much more useful to me alive for now." He points the dagger at Jackson's chest. "Stick to the new plan. Wait for your sister to serve her purpose, then you may kill her."

Chapter 1:
Arrival in Aridel

Soaring Oaks Forest near the City of Aridel

"I wish you would reconsider using the kesseni roots," says Daniel Saveron. "They were rather effective."

Suppressing a sigh, Marina Castaloni nods and makes a neutral noise. They've been over this at least eight times in the last day. She's tried a dozen reassuring responses, and he's come up with as many rebuttals.

"I can't hide who I am forever," she answers softly. She also can't bring herself to imitate her brother, Jackson, in anything, even something as simple as lightening her dark hair to hide her heritage.

"I'm not asking you to hide forever," Daniel says. "Just today, until you're safely in the city." His gaze drifts up and over her left shoulder where the city of Aridel rises, spreading out in rings up the mountainside. "Aridel is a nice city, but it can be harsh with strangers."

She understands that he really means *harsh with Saroth*, but there's no point in bringing up the soaring tensions that exist between their two people. A surge of compassion—and guilt—moves through her. Daniel is not even supposed to be here. By all rights, he should be in Bastion pleading his case before the Arkonai High Council. Every moment's delay hurts his chances the Council will forgive him for not killing her. With much effort, Marina redirects her thoughts to the next task. She must find Kyle's home quickly.

"I should at least see you safely to your friend," Daniel insists. He runs a hand through his light brown hair.

"I'm not sure where to find his house," Marina admits. "It could take me a while to find it, and you can't afford to be seen helping me."

She has enjoyed the past few weeks of traveling with him but letting him escort her into the city would be pure foolishness. Trying to sneak into Aridel isn't exactly her best and brightest move, but Marina needs to see Kyle Ricci. He's perhaps the only man who can help her test the theories about healing through Destroyer Gifts. A pang of regret and loss hits her hard, but she pushes it aside. If she lets it distract her, she might lose the argument and let Daniel risk his life by accompanying her into Aridel.

"I hate leaving you here." Regret and apology flavor Daniel's statement.

"You've done more than enough to fulfill your promise of help," Marina assures him. "Besides, it's still early enough. I can blend in with some Bereft villagers visiting the city." Marina puts more confidence into the words than she's actually feeling.

"I wish I could do more." Daniel lets the sentiment linger a few seconds before clearing his throat nervously, obviously gathering his courage to say something else.

Impulsively, Marina reaches out and catches Daniel's hand. A dozen things she wants to say collide in her head, leaving her speechless. The need to help this Arkonai huntsman causes a strange ache within her chest. If she thought it would do any good, she'd go to Bastion with him to explain what happened. Unfortunately, she can't really explain it to herself, and the Council would likely only imprison or kill her to complete the contract.

"Marina." Daniel's return pressure on her hand is warm, firm, and comforting. "May I place a mark on you?"

"What would that do?" Marina wonders. "Couldn't you do it without my permission?'

He opens his mouth to answer her questions but stops and stiffens at the second one. He drops her hand suddenly and shakes his head.

"Forget it. It's a bad idea," says Daniel. "Forgive me. I'm sorry."

"Forgive what?" Marina smiles, trying to ease him. "I don't even know what you're talking about. There's nothing to apologize for."

"A mark would let me find you easily, no matter where you are on Aeris," Daniel explains. "I want to see you again, but a mark's a bad idea. The Council could use another Seeker to find the mark, even if I tried to hide it."

Marina weighs how she should respond. She wants to convince

him there's no use worrying about such things.

"You're conjuring problems where there may not be any," she says, wincing at borrowing one of her mother's sayings.

"How long will you be in Aridel?" asks Daniel. "I … still want to see you again and help you find your brother."

"If Gabriel has made it home, he should be safe," says Marina. She clings to the words, not fully believing them. Home would place him back in range of Jackson's schemes.

"You're avoiding the question," Daniel notes.

"I can't honestly answer it," says Marina. "I don't want to stay too long, but my friend can help me with some research I've been meaning to do. That might mean a longer stay."

"The Alamon Temple would have a better library of texts to pull from than Aridel," says Daniel. "And it's neutral. You'd be safer."

"I agree in general, but this place likely has more healing texts. Besides, the Temple does not have my friend. I need his knowledge and experience," Marina explains.

"Be safe, Saroth." Daniel sounds worried on her behalf.

Marina bows her head in acknowledgement. When she looks up again, he is gone.

Sneaky Arkonai huntsmen. They're worse than Conjurers. Appearing. Disappearing.

For a short time, Marina stares at the spot where Daniel had stood moments before, expecting him to reappear. Finally, she shakes her head and forces herself to focus. It's not the first time she's been alone. In fact, much of the last few years have been spent alone, traveling between Bereft villages.

You are never truly alone, dear one.

The masculine voice that speaks inside her mind is powerful yet gentle. It doesn't speak often, but Marina likes to think it belongs to the One. It's a nicer sentiment than believing it belongs to a random, unidentified spirit.

Careful observation reveals the general rhythms of travel in and out of Aridel. An imposing wall surrounds the entire city, which has been built atop a mountain. Each ring rises higher than the last, separated from each other by more stone walls. The wide main gates boast the most guards, but they also have the most people entering and exiting. The outer wall also contains several smaller gates at regular intervals. The guards here might be fewer in number, but they tend to check travelers more carefully since there are far fewer of them.

Deciding to take her chances with the main gates, Marina raises the cowl of her dark robes and falls into step several paces behind an elderly Arkonai couple The cut of their clothes is fine enough to tell Marina they're probably from one of the inner rings, though probably not the highest, most exclusive ones.

Her heart beats frantically, but she maintains the slow, casual pace of the Arkonai couple. For their part, the couple appears not to notice anything besides each other. Their heads tilt close together as they hold a whispered conversation. Occasionally, laughter will bubble up out of one or the other. Their clasped hands swing back and forth.

One of the guards nudges the other. They both stand straighter and salute by crossing their right arms across their chests as the couple strolls by. Marina keeps her head ducked as she slips past the guards. Once the couple steps off the main path to approach the next ring, Marina moves away from them.

Now what?

She can't exactly roam the Seventh Ring knocking on doors and hoping to find Kyle. The end of the workday still lies a good hour off. He's probably in the Fourth Ring trying to sell herbs and an assortment of novelty and small task scrolls. The Arkonai might loath almost everything about the Saroth, but they're not above enjoying the entertainment and ease of Minder creations. Marina knows little more than that Kyle has made a decent living procuring special scrolls for his clients.

The surest way to find him would be to seek out his merchant stall, but that would require passing through at least three more gates. Marina settles for making some discreet inquiries and wandering around the Seventh Ring. People here are suspicious by nature, but since most are outcasts themselves, few bother to give her more than a curious glance. Finally, an old, blind woman points Marina toward the gate Kyle should pass through on his way home.

It's on the east side of the city. Since Marina's current location is on the southwest side, she has to jog to reach it.

Arriving as the gate swings shut, Marina's heart sinks.

She's too late. All the merchants are through.

"What are you doing here?"

The familiar deep voice restores Marina's hope. She whirls and embraces her friend.

"Looking for you " she announces.

Kyle Ricci briefly returns the hug before stepping back. A heavy pack slung over one shoulder makes him look like a weary traveler. He frowns down at her.

"Curfew's coming. We must get off the streets," says Kyle. He turns and strides away.

I shouldn't have come.

For the second time in almost as many minutes, Marina feels a pit open in her stomach. Their last correspondence had been strained. Kyle had helped her make arrangements to leave Caramore, but tried his utmost to convince her to stay, despite the fact that his own journey had inspired her to defy her parents' wishes. He had always been like an older brother to her.

"Come on, Sparks. I don't want to lose you."

Kyle's use of the childhood nickname as well as his softened tone comfort her, but it takes a lot of effort for Marina to follow her friend. She's forced to take quick steps to match his long strides. He leads her through several tight paths between rows of community houses until they reach a rundown single-family shack.

"Watch your step. There's a board loose near the door," Kyle warns, pushing the door open and holding it for her. "Welcome to my humble home. It's no estate, but it's all mine."

The statement emphasizes the stark differences between their upbringings. Kyle's family still works a farm on the Castaloni lands. In another few generations, they might be able to buy the land they work, but for now, nothing they own is truly theirs.

"It's very ... you," says Marina, deciding not to lie.

The shack consists of a main room that encompasses bedroom, kitchen, and living space. She assumes the small hallway and two remaining sections to be for facilities and storage. Scrolls and piles of drying herbs cover nearly every flat surface, including much of the floor.

With a laugh, Kyle enters behind Marina and swings the door shut.

"It's a wreck, but thanks anyway," he responds. Crossing over to the only chair, Kyle frees it of the pile of scrolls by brushing them to the floor. "Have a seat. I'll see if the bread from yesterday is still edible. We can eat before I interrogate you on your presence here in one of the most hostile Arkonai strongholds."

"You live here," says Marina. "It can't be too bad."

Kyle pauses with his hand poised above a white cloth covering a basket.

"Marina, we've been over this." Kyle's voice rumbles with

strained patience. "I'm a man, and a lowborn one at that."

"That doesn't matter to me." Marina sinks down onto the chair, suddenly tired of having to fight everybody over every little decision she makes.

"I know, but it matters a great deal to everybody else in this world," says Kyle. "It's not safe for you to travel alone. There are bad people in this world."

"And there are good ones too," Marina counters. "I've met some." Her mind immediately fixes on an image of Daniel.

Kyle groans, sweeps off the white cloth and plucks up a small loaf of bread. Ripping it in half, he tosses the larger chunk to Marina.

"Your idealism is going to get you killed, Sparks," he comments, "but for the record, I'm happy you came. How can I help you?"

Chapter 2:
Before the High Council

Deliverance Hall, City of Bastion

Daniel frowns down at the shiny floor. Every visible surface has been polished to a nearly painful gleam. He thinks back to the first time he stepped foot in these hallowed halls. To be honest, he's almost as nervous now as he was then, but this time, the unease stems from worry rather than excitement.

"They're ready for you," announces Jordan Lekros.

The sound of his friend's voice brings his head up from where it rested in his hands. Daniel quickly comes to his feet and follows as Jordan leads the way through a set of imposing double doors. The chamber beyond the carefully carved doors features a high ceiling that boasts several skylights and a mural of the One's work creating Aeris.

Jordan waves to indicate that Daniel should precede him into the room's center. The chamber is set up like a small arena. Short flights of stairs rise at regular intervals, ascending to the area where the High Council members sit and gaze down upon those brought before them. Today, only five members occupy the nine honor posts. The number of High Council members can fluctuate from time to time, but of the current nine, only a minimum of three are necessary to hold such trials and action reviews. Only five are permanently stationed in the city of Bastion. The others occupy posts in the neutral cities or handle matters from Resilience.

The scribe's pen sits below the Supreme Huntmaster's post, which is close to the center but not in line with the door. The shift happened after a disgruntled huntsman took a shot at one of the past

Council members. Daniel doesn't recognize the scribe, but that's not unusual. The position changes regularly to cut down on the possibility of corruption from that quarter. The section containing benches for spectators is nearly deserted. In fact, the only spectator present is Lady Christa Arrington. Daniel is not sure whether to be relieved or annoyed by the small turnout, but he suspects the Supreme Huntmaster, Christa's uncle, made it a closed session. Even Jordan slips out after escorting Daniel to the appropriate spot.

Daniel quickly scans the Council members, trying to predict where they'll stand concerning his case. Huntmaster Emanuel Ibish of Aridel has always been kind to Daniel. Huntmaster Eric Dillworth and Lord Oleg Wix are known traditionalists who will likely not look favorably upon his actions. The newest member, Lord Asalor Ravine of Urdik isn't known to Daniel, but he'll likely vote exactly as the Supreme Huntmaster does to curry favor. That leaves the Supreme Huntmaster, Ashton Cassel, as the only one Daniel must sway to his cause.

Soon after Daniel takes his place, the Supreme Huntmaster starts the proceedings with a formal statement.

"Huntsman Seeker Daniel Saveron, you have been summoned here to explain your recent actions concerning a silent contract." The Supreme Huntmaster levels a stern gaze at him. "You are aware, of course, that such contracts are extremely rare as they must be personally endorsed by members of this august body."

"I am, sir," answers Daniel, bowing his head contritely.

"Then why would you break such a contract?" demands Lord Asalor Ravine.

The Supreme Huntmaster holds up a hand to quiet the man, but his eyes drill into Daniel, telling him he should answer the question.

"It would have been wrong to fulfill it," says Daniel, knowing they'll demand elaboration despite already having access to the report he submitted upon surrendering to Jordan yesterday.

"Careful, boy,' warns Lord Oleg Wix. "Choose your words wisely. You were sent to hunt down and terminate a Saroth Destroyer. By endorsing the contract, we asked this of you. Why would you break your sacred vows to the Guild?"

"Her name is Marina," Daniel begins.

"Is she a Destroyer?" Huntmaster Eric Dillworth fires the question.

Daniel hesitates but nods to confirm it. Trying to explain the truth would lead to too many dangerous questions.

"Why do you feel fulfilling the contract would have been wrong?" Huntmaster Ibish delivers the question in a direct manner, but there's no ring of accusation to it.

"She didn't start or spread the disease that plagued the village of River's Edge," Daniel says, echoing his report. "Despite being a Destroyer, she tried to help those suffering from Surdan's Bane. Killing her would have been murder, not justice." He bites back a further statement about it being against everything the One and the Lady would want. Still, a warm feeling in his chest confirms the moral rightness of his decision.

All five Council members stare at him. Their expressions range from pity to outright hostility.

"I see," says Huntmaster Ibish. He looks to each of his colleagues in turn. "If this is true, that would be grounds to nullify the contract, assuming of course that it stipulated the Destroyer die because of crimes against River's Edge."

"It did," Daniel assures the huntmaster. "I checked. I did not make my decision lightly."

"I should hope not," comments the Supreme Huntmaster. He too looks to each Council member in turn and receives a subtle nod from both Huntmaster Ibish and Lord Wix. The remaining two stare at him stonily for a second before also giving their approval.

Alarm causes Daniel to tense up. Nothing he can say will change their minds. They must have already discussed the issue at length without him.

Looking relieved, the Supreme Huntmaster gives Daniel a warm smile.

"The nature of a silent contract means that the terms are sealed and inaccessible, even to us, but we believe the matter warrants further investigation," he says.

"Who commissioned the contract?" asks Daniel. Jackson Castaloni might have delivered the contract to Daniel in the guise of Huntmaster Fox, but he wouldn't have the authority to bring the matter before the High Council.

"That doesn't matter," says Lord Wix.

The haste of the protest tells Daniel the likely source.

"Silent contracts exist to safeguard the one who sets them in motion." The gentle reminder comes from Huntmaster Ibish.

"Besides, the knowledge would do you no good."

Unfortunately, he is correct. Even if Daniel had irrefutable proof that Lord Wix had commissioned the contract on Marina's life, it would only lead to more questions without answers. Given the man's fine robes, money was probably his motive, but that wouldn't explain who prompted him to do such a thing in the first place. The ultimate culprit was likely Jackson Castaloni, but that still doesn't explain why a Council member would work with or for the Saroth man.

"We have decided to give you a chance to redeem yourself." The Supreme Huntmaster's announcement pulls Daniel out of his thoughts.

"How so?" Daniel voices the question because he knows it's expected of him. He knows perfectly well what they'll ask of him. His hands form fists at his sides as he prepares to unleash a scathing reply once they present his redeeming task.

"The guilt or innocence of the Destroyer in question will be determined by a separate investigation," explains the Supreme Huntmaster. "But regardless of that outcome, we cannot have a potentially dangerous person loose in our lands."

They want to hold Marina hostage.

Despite the bluster about not being privy to silent contract details, the Council knows exactly who Marina Castaloni is and how valuable she could be to them.

"She is innocent!" Daniel insists. "I was there! I saw her actions, and she did nothing wrong. I swear this by the One and the Lady of Light."

"Your opinion has been noted," says the Supreme Huntmaster. "That does not change our charge to you. Find her and bring her here to tell us the story in her own words."

"No." Daniel's one-word answer contains his disgust at the entire situation. Spinning on his right heel, he takes one step toward the doors, intending to storm out.

"Daniel, please consider their proposal." The plea comes from Lady Christa.

"You are not—"

Lord Asalor gets cut off by the Supreme Huntmaster.

"Let her talk sense into him."

Christa steps smoothly into Daniel's way. He either has to physically knock her aside to pass or dodge around her awkwardly. Instead, he pulls up short and regards his friend carefully. Her hair has been swept up high on her head, but many strands of blond curls cascade down around her shoulders.

"Jordan and I will go with you," says Christa.

"There's nowhere to go *with* me." Daniel barely refrains from growling at his friend. "I'm not going after her. She didn't do anything wrong, and she doesn't deserve to be dragged into political games."

Unshed tears make Christa's eyes glisten. Stepping close, she goes up on tiptoes and braces her hands on his shoulders so she can lean over and whisper in his left ear.

"You must!" Her words are fierce and uncompromising. "I believe you believe in her innocence, but if you don't help them, they will send somebody else. I've read the contract prepared. It demands she be taken alive but grants full authority to use any means necessary to capture and subdue her. You know what that means."

Daniel stiffens with rage, but it's not directed at Christa. The phrasing means that any non-fatal wound can be afflicted in the course of the hunt.

"If you accept the new contract, Jordan and I will be allowed to accompany you," Christa explains. "We'll help you bring her in unharmed. Uncle Ash says she'll get a fair trial."

"You don't believe that." Daniel lets bitterness flow through the words. The trial will go whichever way will most benefit the Council. Bowing his head in acquiescence, Daniel turns away from Christa and faces the High Council. "I want to rewrite the contract before I accept it."

"You should be grateful you're getting a second chance at all," says Lord Wix. "We could do this without your cooperation. Help or head down to the dungeons because those are your only options."

"Breaking a contract is not a confineable offense," says Daniel.

"But defying the High Council is," says the Supreme Huntmaster. "What will it be, huntsman?"

Trembling with the need to hit something, Daniel steps over to the scribe and accepts the enchanted scroll. Each word of the contract becomes clear in his mind. Closing his eyes, he makes several swift changes. First, he makes sure that his friends have an equal share in the contract so they both have the authority to make the arrest. Second, he adds in several clauses to ensure that Marina is the only target so that no one else may be threatened to force her cooperation. Third, he corrects the wording so that she'll be treated with the utmost respect and care throughout the entire event.

The Supreme Huntmaster checks his work and agrees to let the changes stand. Then, the relevant parties sign the contract.

I'm sorry, Marina. I would have never returned if I thought they would pursue you.

Chapter 3:
Family Affairs

Castaloni Estate near the City of Outreach

Jackson Castaloni doesn't need to be a Minder to sense his brother's unease. If the current arrangement gets dissolved, the next most likely match would be between Gabriel and Janine. The meal went surprisingly well, but now that every formality has been met, both families have been gathered to the South drawing room for the main event.

His parents occupy the couch on the room's right side. Their guests, Elena and Pedro Polani sit opposite them. Both couples perch on the edge of their seats. Jackson's assigned chair is located left of his parents. Gabriel sits to his left. There's an empty seat to the right of them that ought to hold Marina. The younger Polani children, Janine and Caleb, flank their parents, right and left respectively. Marcus Polani, the one who insisted upon this meeting, has been given the chair situated between both couches.

Personal guards and servants have been temporarily dismissed, though they're near enough to respond should trouble arise.

"Have you found my betrothed?" demands Marcus Polani. His carefully measured tone does not give many hints as to his true feelings concerning the arrangement.

"We have heard that she has been seen in River's Edge, but that was a few weeks ago," says Father. "Why do you seek her now? There are still almost two years on the contract."

Marcus looks to his parents to see if they want to respond.

"I'm leaving soon to lead an expedition into the Badlands." Pedro Polani reaches out and grasps his wife's hand. "I'd like these matters to be settled before then, so there's no question of succession if the unthinkable happens."

The *unthinkable* means his death, but it takes Jackson a few seconds for the rest of his meaning to sink in. Pedro's younger brother, Roberto, married young and already has four children. The rules of inheritance tend to be straightforward, but there are always loopholes that can be exploited. As the middle child of his own family, Jackson has become an expert on such loopholes. There is a stability clause in most wills. If Pedro dies before Marcus marries, his brother can petition the house council for control of the Polani holdings. The challenge will likely fail, but the possibility explains the urgency to find Marina.

So, don't go. Jackson keeps the words locked inside, but a faint smile from Elena tells him they were probably a very loud thought.

For her part, Elena keeps a tight rein on her emotions. Jackson suspects she's using her Minder Gifts to do so. The youngest Polani child lets his gaze wander the room, clearly bored. Janine simply looks sad.

"I am willing to seek her myself as long as I have your blessing," says Marcus.

"How will you do so?" asks Mother. "I know you are a very talented Minder, but you have never met our daughter."

"I'll help," says Gabriel. "My mind might have similar markings to hers. Besides, I think I know where she'll go next."

Marcus gives Gabriel a grateful nod.

Jackson wants to kick his brother. He does not like the direction of this conversation. He has not yet revealed having forced Marina to give up her Keeper's pendant that would allow her access to Caramore. The contract she signed to purchase the cure for River's Edge effectively forfeited her rights as the firstborn. However, should the circumstances surrounding that incident ever come to light, their father could ignore it and reinstate her as his heir. That's why Marina should have died that day. If Marcus finds her, brings her back, and marries her, Jackson's chances of gaining his rightful inheritance will disappear. He would inherit on paper upon his father's death, but in practicality, the power and wealth would go to Marina's second child in the long run.

"I will help too," Jackson offers, knowing he must reach Marina first.

Without contact, Marina would likely be perfectly content to spend the rest of her days wandering Aeris mixing herbal remedies for destitute Bereft. But her do-gooder heart also contains deep streaks of duty. Marcus's tale of woe might be enough to convince her to accept her responsibilities and return to Caramore.

"You can't both go," says Father. "I need one of you to stay and continue your studies."

Jackson reconsiders. The search will probably be tedious and frustrating, and he might never get such an opportunity to work alongside his father.

"As you wish, Father," says Jackson. "Gabriel can go."

He sends a significant look his brother's way. Gabriel *will* keep him well-informed of the search party's progress. Getting him out of Caramore will be good too. The threat against Tielle has been effective in controlling him so far, but the recent events have placed a further strain on their relationship. If he pushes too far, Gabriel might snap and spill the entire story to Father. That would be disastrous.

"It's settled then," says Father.

"Not quite." Pedro's statement has an ominous edge to it.

"If we are committed to uniting our houses, we should come up with a secondary contract," explains Elena. "I have prepared one for you to consider." She nods to her younger son.

The boy snaps his fingers tentatively a few times. On the fifth try, he manages to open a small tear in the Veil and withdraw a scroll. He promptly hands the item over to his mother, beaming at the small triumph.

Marcus collects the scroll from his mother and walks it over to Mother and Father.

Jackson doesn't need to see it. The furtive glances Janine keeps shooting at Gabriel tell him more than enough.

"It has much the same terms as the original contract for Marcus and Marina," says Elena. "There are a few changes to compensate for the shift in significance given that neither Janine nor Gabriel is likely to control the entirety of our respective household businesses."

"That won't be necessary," Gabriel declares. "We'll find my sister."

"But will she abide by the contract?" asks Pedro. "She knew about the arrangement soon after it was made, and instead of returning home, she went to the farthest corner of the continent."

"Marina has always been headstrong," says Father, "but she also knows her duties. I'm certain when the situation is explained to her, she'll come around."

Jackson doubts his father's speech has much impact upon the Polani elders. The meeting's existence proves that both families are committed to the union. The Polani name might be more prestigious, but a few poor decisions—including Pedro's obsession with hunting Darkland artifacts in the Badlands—have left the businesses in a sad state. The Castaloni wealth would certainly improve things for them. In turn, the Polani name would open new avenues and opportunities to expand businesses greatly.

I could do a lot with the power of that name.

For an insane moment, Jackson considers offering to marry Janine himself. The age gap of nine years might be significant now, but such things will matter less in the future. First, Jackson must sort the Marina problem and secure the inheritance. Then, he can worry about expanding the holdings. If everything goes well with his original plans, he can force Gabriel to marry the girl and gain the connections without the nuisance of a wife. To secure his place, he'll eventually have to marry and produce heirs, but if Gabriel marries Janine, Jackson will be free to target higher houses like the Capone or Puchini families. Too bad the main line of the Seriano family only has boys.

"Who else will travel with you?" asks Mother, directing the question to Marcus with her eyes.

"A friend and one other," he answers.

"We think it best to keep the party small and unobtrusive," explains Elena. "Marcus has a friend who recently completed his first year of training with the Nokarti Assassins. Adaram Serco should be able to provide them with some protection."

"The last member should be a Minder with tracking abilities or a Shapeshifter to act as a scout, but we've not found a suitable candidate yet," adds Pedro.

"Gabriella Ricci's a Minder," Gabriel points out. "She was always good at finding things when we were kids."

Jackson looks hard at his brother, trying to fathom a motive for mentioning the girl. Sharing male and female forms of the same name had drawn the pair together despite a significant age gap, but Mother's strict oversight kept the friendship from developing into more.

"I'm sure she's too busy with her training," says Mother. She had essentially sent both Ricci siblings away when they got too close.

Kyle became a successful merchant in Aridel largely due to Mother's initial patronage. Gabriella was sent to the Alamon Temple to train with Minder Gera Patros.

"She'll help if she can," Gabriel assures everybody. "Besides, her half-brother is a good friend of Marina's. They have the same father but different mothers. Even if Kyle Ricci has not seen Marina, he probably knows her better than any of us. If any soul could predict where she'd go next, it's him."

"Perfect," says Pedro Polani. "I'll have my staff draft the proposal to hire this young Minder. If anybody questions them, they can claim to be escorting her to meet her half-brother."

"May we proceed with the preparations?" asks Marcus, speaking to Mother and Father.

Mother nods curtly, but Father lets several seconds of awkward silence build up.

"You may if you can answer one question to my satisfaction," says Father. "What will you do if our daughter flatly refuses to return with you?"

Every eye fixes upon Marcus. It's a moral and legal question. The betrothal contract is backed up with magical enchantments which would compel Marina to return with him regardless of her personal feelings on the matter. Even if she appealed to the Tariku League itself, Marina would have a hard time breaking the contract if Marcus used it to full effect.

"I … hope I can convince her to consider building a relationship with me," answers Marcus. He stands stiffly between both sets of parents with hands clasped behind his back like a man on trial. He looks solemnly at Father. "But I will not compel her to become my wife if she is unwilling. That is no way to start a life together."

"Good answer," says Father. "You have our blessing to find Marina and present yourself to her."

Jackson isn't certain whether he ought to wish success or failure upon the mission. He needs them to find Marina, but he cannot allow her to step foot in Caramore as a married woman. Even her lack of a Keeper's pendant wouldn't matter if she travels through the barrier in the presence of her husband.

As the conversation turns to other matters, Jackson lets his thoughts wander. If only he'd been born first, he wouldn't have to work so hard to obtain what should belong to him. They would still not be friends since Marina follows the One almost as devoutly as Father, but it would make her tolerable. In a way, he should be grateful her rebellious streak has led her away from being the dutiful heir.

I don't hate you, dear sister, but I need you dead to claim what's mine.

Chapter 4:
Dangerous and Delicate

Home of Kyle Ricci, City of Aridel

The last hour before Kyle returns from his merchant duties stretches on painfully long for Marina. She hates being confined to the tiny house, but she had promised to stay in while he worked.

At night, they shared adventures like sneaking out of the city to gather herbs or exploring the quiet places within Aridel. The Arkonai had some strange notions, but Marina enjoyed learning about them. The huntsmen stationed in the city took regular shifts guarding the various gates between the rings and enforcing the curfew. Time in Bereft villages had introduced her to the idea of a curfew, but it still struck her as strange. In Caramore, the general rhythms of individual cities dictated who could go where safely and at what times of day or night. The Shadow Army spent most of its time training and dealing with dangers that arose in the Ashlands and the Badlands. It had no time to mind the comings and goings of the people.

Tonight's adventure would be quite different. Throughout the past week, they had made discrete inquiries into those who had diseases or ailments the Healers could not—or would not—mend. Marina had spent the entire day preparing the tiny house to function as a clinic. The table had been moved into the main section, and the many dozens of scrolls and herbs had been sorted, categorized, and stored along the walls. They had only invited one person, but if tonight went well, they had plans for building a separate room on to the house.

With the work done, Marina has enough time to think, pray, and pace, a habit she picked up while studying at the Alamon Temple.

Lady of Light, bless the work we intend to do this night. May our efforts bring glory to the One. Help us. Help me. I ... need to prove that Destroyers weren't only meant for destruction. Our Gifts come from the One. They can bring about good.

A knock pulls Marina out of her thoughts. She stops pacing and stares at the door. A wave of nervousness washes through her. Three steps bring her to the door. She longs to swing it open wide and welcome the guest, but caution prevails.

"Who calls this night?" she inquires.

"One who seeks aid," answers a female voice.

Satisfied, Marina opens the door and ushers the lady inside. Taking the woman's left elbow, she guides the guest over to the single chair and settles her upon it.

"Can I get you anything?" asks Marina, trying to keep her voice steady. There's precious little she can offer the woman, except maybe a cup of water. Kyle brings fresh bread from the market each day, but he has not yet returned.

"Goodness, child. You sound more nervous than I am," notes the woman. Serena Beri speaks in an unhurried manner that emphasizes the refined accent Marina has come to expect from the Arkonai. "I am fine, but while we have a moment, tell me what brings you to the Seventh Ring? This place has always attracted the hopeless."

"My friend lives here," says Marina. "We wish to provide some hope to those who have none." Doubts assail her, prompting her to warn the lady. "But I know it can be dangerous and delicate work. We've never done this before. Are you sure you want us to attempt a cure for your ailment?"

"I may be blind, but I am rather fond of living," says Serena. "I have been to countless Healers. They have no satisfactory answers for me. If you do nothing, I will likely pass beyond the Veil in a matter of weeks. So, you have already succeeded in your task of bringing hope."

"But what if we hurt you?" The question slips out as Marina's mind fills with reasons they should reconsider their whole plan. If they were in Caramore, a very thorough contract would be written, reviewed, and signed by both parties before such a transaction could take place.

"I doubt you could do much worse than I experience each day." Serena speaks with little emotion.

"I'm sorry you've had to go through that," says Marina. A thought occurs to her. "May I ask how you came to lose your sight?"

"When this unknown disease came upon me, my vision grew

blurrier each day until I opened my eyes to darkness," says Serena.

Marina nods, but then realizes the woman can't see the silent response.

"If it's related to the disease, we might be able to reverse the effects," she reasons, "but I don't want to give you false hope."

Kyle's arrival lifts the somber mood settling upon them. He takes over the duties of preparing the woman for the treatment by serving her a sleeping draught. Before it kicks in, he helps her up onto the table, which has one of his blankets thrown on top.

While they wait for the woman to sleep, Marina has a quick meal. It takes a lot of effort to eat, but the night could stretch on very long. Kyle will be doing most of the work, but Marina's mind must be sharp throughout the process so she can troubleshoot problems that arise.

At last, they are ready to begin. They stand on opposite sides of the table and stare at each other.

"Your move, Sparks," says Kyle. "Tell me what to do."

"When I spoke with her at length about the disease, she said it started on the right side of her stomach," says Marina. "I guess that's the best place to start."

Kyle gives her an uncertain look.

"You want me to touch her there?" he asks.

Heat creeps up Marina's neck and cheeks.

"Yes, touching her is going to be important for the work," Marina answers dryly. She smiles sympathetically at the awkward position she's placed her friend in. Steeped in formality and tradition, Saroth culture has much to say about proper interactions between men and women. Touching the stomach of a complete stranger falls into the taboo category, but Marina admits most of her ideas do much the same.

My presence as a guest in Kyle's home isn't exactly the definition of propriety.

"I probably should have had her change into a nightshift," Marina muses.

"Do you have a spare one?" Kyle crosses his arms while he waits for her reply.

Marina looks from the woman on the table then back up at her friend, brow knit in concentration.

"What's that look for?" demands Kyle. "I do not like that look."

"Do you have any clean shirts?" Marina wonders. "None of my clothes will fit her, and we probably shouldn't destroy the one outfit she owns."

Kyle's expression still reads dubious, but he digs through the box where he keeps spare clothes until he finds a large white shirt. The woman's current attire consists of a filthy dress that has been patched many times and cloth wrappings over much of her arms and legs.

It takes Marina and Kyle several minutes to carefully unwind the rags. Dirt and dust come off the wrappings in clumps. As the first falls free, Marina gasps then almost chokes as her stomach twists at the sight. The upper portion of the woman's left arm is covered in large red welts. A few bulge. One has even split open.

Tears sting Marina's eyes.

"We have to help her." She whispers the statement, but it booms throughout the quiet house. Her heart longs to find and destroy whatever has brought Serena so much suffering.

Without another word, Kyle and Marina work together to free the woman from her old clothes and pull the clean white shirt over her head and into place. Since none of his pants would fit the lady anyway, they drape another blanket over the lower half of her body. Sweating from the labor, they carefully lift the shirt up and fold it across Serena's chest, exposing her stomach. A strange, red rash covers most of the skin along the right side of her body.

Marina wants to turn away or cover up the wounds and run, but too many people have done exactly that to this poor woman.

"Place your hands on the affected area, and tell me what you feel," Marina instructs. A surge of doubt stabs her. Before committing to this path, they discussed the possibilities of contracting any of the diseases they mean to combat. Marina's usual answer for such a question would be to turn to the books and scrolls on the topic. But there are none because Destroyers have never applied their Gifts this way before.

Carefully, Kyle places both hands over the rash and closes his eyes.

"The skin is warm but not overly feverish. It's an unnatural warmth though," he reports.

"Do you sense anything wrong?" asks Marina. "A darkness. Something out of place." Her theories hold that the root cause of certain physical ailments is spiritual. At the core, Destroyer Gifts have much to do with the spirit realms bleeding over into the natural world.

"I'm not sure what I'm feeling," Kyle admits. "I don't think I've ever tried to feel another's spirit this way before."

"Maybe a comparison will help," says Marina. "Try reading me first. What do I feel like to you?" She holds both hands out to her friend, palms down.

Lifting his hands to meet hers, Kyle once again closes his eyes. His spirit touch is clumsy at first, like a blind man feeling his way through a room by swinging his arms from left to right.

Concentrating, Marina tries to relax and remove any mental obstacles Kyle might encounter.

For several seconds, they simply stand there, hands clasped above Serena's prone form. Although she tries to keep her spirit open and passive, curiosity drives Marina to reach out and sense her friend. The impressions she receives remind her of freshly cut cedar wood, a crisp autumn evening, and rocky, snowcapped mountains. She lacks the time to thoroughly interpret the images, but she gathers that they represent his strength and bright sense of vitality. Part of Marina wishes to extend the current moment, but she knows Serena still needs their help. Reluctantly, she pulls back her hands.

Kyle returns his attention to Serena and takes up a similar pose to the one he struck earlier with both hands touching the rash upon her right side.

"She feels different, but that's to be expected," he says at last. "I can tell you're healthier, but you're also younger."

"Let me try," offers Marina. "I might not be able to access my Destroyer Gifts, but I felt your spirit. I can probably sense hers as well."

They switch places.

As soon as her hands touch the woman's side, Marina feels the faint unnatural warmth Kyle mentioned.

Holy Father, let me find what I seek.

Following a feeling, Marina stretches out with her spirit and moves her attention slowly over the woman's entire body. The unaffected parts of Serena feel like soft white light. The parts that are swollen with disease feel like various colors ranging from black to deep red. Lifting her hands off Serena's stomach, Marina describes the impressions to Kyle.

Gesturing for one of his hands, Marina places it over one of the darkest spiritual spots.

"There's nothing there," he protests. "The skin here is healthy."

"On the outside," Marina agrees, "but look within."

He does so.

Marina watches his expression rapidly morph from confusion to surprise to determination.

"Do you sense it?"

"I do," he replies.

"That is our enemy. Destroy it." The command flows out of Marina without any hesitation.

Over the course of several hours, they continue working together to identify each section. Eventually, they recognize that most of the areas that look normal harbor the tiny entities that don't belong. After painstakingly isolating and destroying each, Kyle moves his attention to Serena's eyes.

He finds nothing spiritually wrong.

Once again, Marina prays for wisdom.

Have we saved this woman only to leave her in darkness?

What is your request, dear one?

The warm, compassionate male voice resonates in her heart and mind.

Please, restore the light to her eyes.

Your faith has made you strong. Do not fear to use the Gifts granted to you but understand that everything has a cost.

The words aren't exactly comforting this time, but Marina weighs them and accepts them.

"Kyle, I need your help," says Marina. Her voice sounds dry and hoarse. "What I intend to do requires great strength, more than I possess. I can draw the difference from you, if you are willing." Quickly, Marina describes what she needs to do.

"I am willing," says Kyle, holding out his right hand to her.

Without hesitation, Marina grips the hand with her left and places her other hand over Serena's closed eyes. Then, she reaches for the magic within. Yellow light passes from her hand into the woman's eyes. Marina feels power leave her and return several times. Each time, she feels weaker. It's over in seconds, but by the end, her head pounds and her vision darkens.

She collapses forward.

Kyle catches her shoulders and eases her down across Serena's chest.

Marina is dimly aware of Kyle moving around the table until he steps up beside her. Pulling her off Serena, Kyle picks Marina up and moves her over to the bed.

"I think that's enough healing for today, Sparks. Get some sleep."

As she drifts off to sleep, Marina sees Kyle sink wearily onto the chair beside the bed.

Chapter 5:
A Desperate Plan

Kyle Ricci's House, Seventh Ring, City of Aridel

As he races toward the tiny place holding Marina, Daniel reaches out with his Seeker Gifts to gain a sense of the situation. He sent Tegan, Christa's stable boy, to fetch her and Jordan from the Gathering Hall where they had gone to alert the city council of their intent to make an arrest soon, but they will never arrive in time to help.

Four hooded figures broke through the door mere seconds ago.

Although he cannot read them well enough to identify them, Daniel feels their dark intent. His Gifts allow him to track each presence as the four hostile figures surround one male and two female presences near the room's center. Two move toward the male presence while the other two converge on one of the females, pulling her off to the side.

As he crosses the threshold, Daniel pauses long enough to summon a short sword from the Veil. His preferred weapon, a bow, would be useless in such tight quarters.

"Stop!" Daniel pours as much conviction into the command as he can muster. He has always fared well in single combat contests, but if he lets it devolve into a fight, somebody will die.

Each attacker wears a cloth mask that encompasses his entire face, save a small opening to allow him to see. One man holds the shoulders of a tall, dark-skinned man, while the other punches him in the face. This must be Marina's friend Kyle. The other pair adjusts to deal with Daniel's arrival. The nearest man whirls and brandishes a pair of shiny daggers. The man behind him has Marina in a tight chokehold, one arm looped around her neck and the other around her stomach. Her hands clutch at the arm encircling her neck to no avail. He has no weapon that Daniel can see, but he also doesn't need any. If he maintains his grip, she'll lose consciousness soon.

"Let her go," says Daniel, raising his sword to a guard position. He slides sideways to gain the most space in case there's a fight.

"Leave and you get to live," says the man directly in front of him.

Now that he's closer to the attackers, Daniel senses the youthfulness in their spirits.

"This is none of your business, huntsman," adds another man. He flexes his hand, which probably hurts from having recently punched the other prisoner. "We're simply loyal citizens cleansing our great city. Go learn to conjure a new weapon or something."

The bitterness in the man's voice tells Daniel he probably tried to join the Arkonai Hunting Guild and failed somewhere along the way.

"It is my business," Daniel says, barely keeping his anger in check. "I have a contract to fulfill, and you're holding her." His eyes pierce the man who has his arms wrapped tightly around Marina.

"Is there a reward?" asks the man. He loosens his hold slightly.

Marina's eyes are clenched shut, but the grip she has on the arm across her neck has slackened.

"We're not giving you anything," declares the leader. He glares at the man holding Marina. "These Saroth dared to step foot in our beautiful city and do unnatural things to innocent people. We won't stand for it!"

"Please, don't do this!" The plea comes from the young woman Daniel clearly forgot about. Her accent says she's likely from one of the Bereft villages nearby. Long blond hair flows down her back and skims the top of the table she sits upon. She wears only a white nightshift. He can't see her face because her it's angled away from him.

"Everything's fine, ma'am. We won't let them hurt you," says the leader gently. He offers the lady a hand and helps her climb off the table.

The woman nods thanks, but then regards the leader curiously.

"They weren't harming me," she says, removing her hands from the man's grasp. "I came ta them for help."

Kyle shakes his head, trying to catch her attention. His eyes beg the woman to tell the attackers what they want to hear.

"Is that so." The leader's tone darkens. He takes a small, menacing step toward her.

Knowing the others are distracted, Daniel slips around the man with the daggers and the one holding Marina. He brings the point of his sword to the center of the man's back.

"You will release her right now." Daniel lets his anger burn through the order. He probably wouldn't stab through the man for fear of killing Marina too, but this man doesn't know that.

Instead of simply letting Marina go, the man gives her a hard shove. She stumbles at the attacker with the daggers. He knocks her down by driving the back end of his left dagger hard into her right shoulder. Daniel hears her breath rush out as her back hits the floor.

A cry escapes the Bereft woman, but the leader's hand upon her shoulder prevents her from moving to help Marina. Daniel kicks his prisoner's right leg and forces the man to kneel. His sword rests on the man's right shoulder and his other hand has a firm grip on the man's shirt. The dagger-wielder kneels over Marina and rests the crossed blades over her throat.

"Do you have her?" calls the leader. The table prevents him from seeing them.

Daniel has a clear view of all three crises.

"I have her," confirms the man.

"Good. Get her up. We'll finish this elsewhere," says the leader. "Huntsman, let my friend up, unless you want their blood spilled—"

Instead of finishing the thought, the man sways and staggers against the table. His arms tremble with the effort to hold his weight upright. The man holding Kyle shoves him forward, spins right, and sprints to the door. He nearly crashes into the dagger-wielder who is also trying to exit as quickly as possible.

"Let the man go and he will leave." The female voice that speaks within Daniel's mind sounds tense and exhausted.

He feels a pressure inside his head and suspects that the thought is not a request. While he ponders his options, Daniel watches with a mixture of horror and fascination as Marina, Kyle, and the Bereft woman fall asleep before his eyes. Against his better judgment, Daniel obeys the voice in his head. Swinging his sword away from the man's neck, Daniel tugs on his shirt to get him to stand.

"Do not return to this place," he warns, gesturing toward the door with the sword.

Even the leader is gone by now. The fourth man races for the exit.

Stretching out with his Seeker Gifts, Daniel is surprised to feel three more male presences and one female emerging from the tiny back room. Even with the distraction of recent events, his Gifts should have revealed the additional people hiding in the back room. Either they weren't there before, or a very powerful Minder had concealed them. Lowering his sword to a non-threatening position, Daniel studies the newcomers.

All four have dark hair and lean, fit forms. The first man's confident stride declares him to be the leader. The second man is Gabriel Castaloni, Marina's younger brother. The woman must be the Minder, for her presence shines brighter than the others now that she has dropped the shield. The third man keeps to the background, but his subtle movements tell Daniel he's likely the party's strongest fighter.

"What did you do to them?" Daniel asks. He directs the question to the woman but keeps his eyes upon Marina's still form. He wants to check on her but dares not drop his guard yet.

"There isn't much time," says the first man.

"Your friends are coming," explains the Minder.

"My name is Marcus Polani," continues the first man, speaking swiftly. "You already know Gabriel Castaloni. My other companions are Gabriella Ricci and Adaram Serco. We came to take Marina back to Caramore, but I see that's going to be more complicated than anticipated."

"Why?" asks Daniel. "Step through any of the portals to neutral ground. Don't you have Teleportation scrolls?"

The Minder moves to Kyle and checks on him. The strong resemblance between them becomes apparent when they're side by side. Despite the difference in their skin tones, their spirits feel similar enough to mark them as siblings.

Daniel tenses as Gabriel moves to Marina's side.

"I'm not here to hurt her," the young man assures him.

"Hard to believe. The last time I—" Daniel begins.

"Huntsman, please, listen. Time is very short," says Gabriella. "They will awaken soon, and our path must be set before then."

"Why?" asks Daniel again. More of his frustration comes through the question this time. "What's complicated about this? Take her and go. Don't tell me where. Just disappear."

"You have a contract to fulfill," Gabriel reminds Daniel. The young man kneels next to his sister and gently rests a hand on her left shoulder. "She would never forgive us if we stole her away and left you to die."

"Let me handle my Council," says Daniel. Their assumption that the High Council would kill him for breaking a second contract annoys him even though it's a valid concern.

"There's no need for that," answers Marcus. "Don't you sense the larger problem?" He waves down to Marina's still form.

With a sinking heart, Daniel focuses his Gifts upon Marina and finally senses the mark placed upon her. One of the attackers, likely the one waving daggers about, must have possessed some Seeker abilities. The mark is bright, clumsy, and easy to find but effective. It will fade in time, but for now, that means the attackers can find her anywhere on Aeris if they have the skill to follow the mark. Daniel might be able to mask it or weaken it, but he cannot completely undo the mark. Only a Seeker Master can destroy another's mark.

"Can you do something?" Daniel looks to the Minder for an answer.

"Not yet," replies the Minder, rising gracefully to her feet. "If given enough time, I might be able to learn how to answer for it, but I do not currently have that knowledge."

"There are very few places she'll be safe while we wait for that mark to fade," Marcus explains.

"We must get her to Temperance," says Daniel. "That's the nearest neutral ground."

"They would follow." This statement comes from the man keeping to the background.

"Who are they?" wonders Daniel. "What prompted the attack?"

"Those are good questions for later," answers Marcus. "For now, I believe we can help each other."

"How so?" Realizing he still has his sword in hand, Daniel sends it back into the Veil.

"Keep my sister safe." The answer comes from Gabriel.

"We need you to make the arrest," says Marcus. He nods to indicate that Gabriella should pick up the explanation.

"After that, you must convince your friend, Lady Christa Arrington, to place Marina in protective custody and let her stay in her family home." Gabriella's gaze becomes distant, and she stops speaking.

Daniel never would have conceived of such a plan on his own, but it might work. Making the arrest will fulfill his obligation for the Council, freeing him from the contract. Soaring Oaks, Christa's childhood home, is well-protected because it's part of the First Ring, the highest and most exclusive section of Aridel.

"We're having a Keeper's pendant forged for her, but that won't be ready for a few weeks." Marcus looks at Daniel uncertainly. "Without this, she won't be able to enter Caramore as a citizen. Do you think your friend will agree to safeguard her that long?"

"Of course, she will," Daniel answers without hesitation. A new thought makes him wince. "But her uncle is the Supreme Huntmaster, and if he finds out, there would be a whole new set of problems. Marina cannot fall into Council hands."

"Agreed," says Marcus. "Once the mark fades and the Keeper's pendant is ready, we'll make arrangements to remove her from the city."

"How are we going to get her up to Christa's home?" Daniel wonders.

"Jordan and Tegan are fetching some horses," Christa announces as she enters the tiny house. Spotting Daniel, she adds, "You keep interesting company, Daniel."

The Saroth men straighten and bow formally to Lady Christa.

"I will explain more fully later if you like, Lady Arrington," offers Gabriella, confirming Daniel's guess that Christa knows the situation.

"I suspect the less I know the better," says Christa. "Daniel can fill me in later. The rest of you should get moving."

In answer to the question written on Daniel's face, Gabriella explains Christa's cryptic statement.

"The attackers you faced tonight belong to the Arkonai Brotherhood."

Daniel frowns. He always considered them to be a gang of disgruntled fools.

"We're going to draw them away," says Gabriella. She directs a sad look at her unconscious half-brother.

"How will you do that?" asks Christa.

"Now that I have a sense for the mark placed upon Marina, I can imitate it." Gabriella's expression dares Daniel to question the plan.

He finally understands her expression.

"It's too dangerous," he protests.

"I have my protectors," Gabriella assures him with a tight smile. "And I will turn it off as soon as you and Lady Christa tell me Marina is safe."

"Huntsman, you must go with them in case this doesn't work." Marcus's tone declares the unease within him.

"How will we know you're safe?" asks Daniel.

"When Marina awakens, you will know we are safe … or dead," answers Gabriella. "Blessings of the One be with you."

Almost as swiftly as they appeared, the four Saroth file out.

Gabriel pauses in the threshold and pulls a small scroll from the folds of his dark robes.

"Please give th_s to Marina when she wakes up," says Gabriel. "And tell her I'm sorry ... for everything."

Chapter 6:
Harsh Reminders

Castaloni Estate near the City of Dominance, Caramore

"You wanted to speak with me, sir?" asks Tielle Toscano, cautiously entering the door to Jackson's private study. She stays near the door, keeping one hand upon it to hold it open.

"I did," says Jackson. "Please, come in. I have a matter of deep importance to discuss with you." Waving her over to a comfortable set of chairs, Jackson indicates that she should be seated.

As she moves closer, Jackson uses a spell from a scroll to brighten the four energy orbs scattered around the room. This allows him to see the curiosity shining behind Tielle's captivating, light green eyes. Another spell closes the door and locks it. Jackson doesn't like being so dependent upon scrolls made by others, but he's no Minder. He can't risk being caught at this stage, but there's also very little chance he would encounter Tielle elsewhere. She only comes to this estate once every other week to train with his mother for a few hours before returning to her parents' farm.

"Did you enjoy the lesson today?" Jackson inquires, keeping his tone light and pleasant. "What did you learn?"

Tielle nods.

"We worked on multiplying bread," says the girl. She sits on the edge of a chair, looking nervously back at the door. Her lips form a slight frown as she turns her gaze back to Jackson.

The girl's statement reminds Jackson of his first Conjuring lessons. That brings up thoughts of his master, August Polani, which ignites frustration within him. The old man was happy enough to cultivate his Gifts through the mundane aspects, but he refuses to teach Jackson anything useful, except the ability to conjure oneself from place to place. If his master cannot provide the necessary lessons soon, Jackson will have to move on, but first, he'll have to find out where the old man keeps his ancient texts.

A problem for another day.

"Is Master Gabriel around?" asks Tielle.

Her hopeful question pulls Jackson out of his thoughts.

"He will be soon," Jackson promises.

It's true in a way. Gabriel is scheduled to make a call through his Keeper's pendant soon, but they still have a few minutes.

"Before then, I want to clarify some things with you," says Jackson. Without warning, he releases the last two spells he had prepared for the evening: a privacy shield and a binding spell. The first causes the air around them to shimmer. For the next half-hour, nothing said within the room will escape. The second causes the ropes Jackson had hidden underneath the chair to go to their preassigned locations. Part wraps tightly around Tielle's legs while the other immobilizes her arms by pinning them to her sides.

She grunts as the air rushes from her lungs. Anger flashes in her eyes as she thrashes, trying to break free. The movement brings her up off the chair.

Catching her, Jackson pushes her back into place.

The anger flips over to terror, rendering her speechless.

"I don't require a response from you yet, but do listen closely," says Jackson. "I couldn't care less that my brother has his heart set on you. He's not a threat to me, but I do have a sister, an older sister. The laws are such that she will inherit everything upon my father's death unless I can remove her as a threat. You're going to help me with this problem."

Tielle shakes her head.

"Lady Marina was always kind to me," she protests.

"She probably doesn't know you exist," Jackson says honestly.

The girl was likely only a child when Marina left home to study at the Alamon Temple several years ago. She never returned from those studies. She might never return, but Jackson cannot take that chance.

"Focus on the consequences of not helping me," instructs Jackson. Unconsciously, he straightens into a lecturing pose picked up from Master Polani. "You too have a sister, a younger one, and I'm assuming you care for my brother. I will kill them both."

"But why?" The question bursts out of Tielle as tears pool in her eyes. "You said Gabriel's not a threat to you."

She doesn't mention her sister, but a glance toward the door tells Jackson she's thinking of Daria.

"He's not," Jackson confirms, "but he's also not enthusiastic about helping me. I need you to change his mind about that, but it is not your primary task."

Confusion sweeps over Tielle's face.

"As you said, Lady Marina hardly knows me, what could I possibly say to her that would wield any sort of influence upon her?" Her voice steadies as she focuses on Jackson.

"It's not who you are, but what you'll say that matters," Jackson assures her. "I'm going to give you a Teleportation scroll and a short privacy scroll. When the time comes, I need you to visit my dear sister and deliver a message." He pauses to lock eyes with Tielle and confirm that she's listening closely. "If she ever returns to Caramore, I will kill our brother."

"You can't," declares Tielle. "The house council would exile you."

"They'll never know it's me," says Jackson. "That knowledge stays between you and me."

"If he's dead, you'll have no hold on me." Tielle lifts her chin and glares at Jackson.

He shrugs, not bothering to tell her about the privacy spell.

"Your sister's life should be hold enough. Besides, I'll deny it. Who do you think they'll believe?" Jackson tilts his head, letting her think about that.

The question saps some of her defiance.

"Why can't you deliver the awful message yourself?" Tielle wonders.

"Because I believe you will be much more persuasive," answers Jackson. "You love him, do you not?"

"Of course, but what prevents you from carrying out your threat even if she obeys? What kind of future can we have?" The second question is soft with desperation.

Kneeling before Tielle, Jackson picks up one of her hands and squeezes it.

"I do not want to harm anybody," he says. "Once I have what is mine, Gabriel will receive his due, and you can live in peace."

His blue Keeper's pendant warms, telling him that Gabriel will be connected to him soon.

"Ah, there he is now," comments Jackson, regaining his feet. He takes a second to pull her upright on the chair. "Let me explain things to him."

"Explain what?' Gabriel asks.

"Are you alone? ' Jackson demands.

"For the moment," Gabriel replies, sounding irritated. "What's so important?"

"I don't think you're taking me seriously, so I arranged for Tielle to join me this evening," answers Jackson.

"Stay away from her!" shouts Gabriel. "She's—"

"Already involved," says Jackson, smoothly interrupting his brother. "Would you like to speak with her?"

"Jack, there's no reason to drag her into this!" Gabriel protests. "Please, I know what you want, and I'll help you get it. I promise. Tell me what I can do."

"That's better, but I still think you should hear from her." Jackson removes the Keeper's pendant from around his neck and holds it out toward his prisoner. "Try out your persuasive skills, Tielle."

"Gabriel, you should stay away!" calls Tielle. "He says he'll kill you!"

Conjuring a clean rag, Jackson stuffs it into Tielle's mouth.

"That is not what I said," he counters.

A muffled noise comes from Tielle, but she cannot dislodge the gag.

"What did you do?' Gabriel demands. "If you hurt her, I'll—"

"Remember, you can't do anything significant," says Jackson.

"I'll testify before the house council," Gabriel threatens.

"You'll only condemn yourself as well," replies Jackson. Despite the nonchalant words, the desperation in Gabriel worries him. He needs his brother to obey, not quit.

Silence falls between them.

"Why are we doing this?" Gabriel wonders at last. "I don't even think you have anything to worry about concerning Marina. She looks happy here, and she's made it clear she wants no part of running the holdings."

"I'm not leaving anything to chance," says Jackson.

"If she marries Marcus, you'll win." Gabriel's voice is earnest. "Father will have no choice but to name you heir."

"Marina is not going to marry Marcus for any monetary reason."

Jackson's utterly surprised that Gabriel can't see the truth.

As the third child, he never bothered researching the matter as thoroughly as Jackson, so he probably doesn't even know about the secondary succession clause.

Jackson doesn't bother explaining it to his brother, but it means that everything would revert to Marina's second child should he or she choose to fully embrace their Castaloni heritage when they come of age.

"There's a slim chance she'll actually fall for him once they meet, but that's unlikely," says Jackson. "Can you honestly see her becoming a Polani matron?"

"No, but I never imagined you trying to kill her over this stupid inheritance either." Gabriel's tone is bitter. "Is it worth destroying every tie to your family?"

The question pierces Jackson. He doubts the Dark Man would even let him back out on their deal now, but the quest to prove himself worthy has been challenging—and lonely—so far.

"Sacrifices must be made," he says. Hardening his tone, he continues, "I must cut this heart-to-heart short, so pay attention. Tielle will return to her parents soon. Everybody will go about their business as usual. You both have your assignments."

"What do you want her to do?" Gabriel asks.

"I'll let her explain, if she'll be honest with you," says Jackson. He shoots the girl a significant look and slowly reaches for the gag.

"I'm supposed to tell your sister of his threat against you," Tielle explains. Her voice is suitably subdued. "If she returns, he says he will kill you."

"And her," adds Jackson. "And you and your sister and anyone else I think you've ever cared about." He directs the last part to Tielle with a tight smile. "Everybody dies if Marina returns. If she stays away and I get my inheritance, you two can go wherever you wish. Marina can live out her days anywhere on Aeris, except Caramore."

"Jack, we should be focusing on keeping our family strong, not tearing it apart," pleads Gabriel. "Especially now that Father's fallen ill." His breath hitches and his next statement comes out barely audible. "Tell me you have nothing to do with that."

"I have nothing to do with that," Jackson lies easily. "Do you think I'd really harm Father before the inheritance question is settled in my favor?"

"I guess not," Gabriel admits.

Jackson stares down at the Keeper's pendant, giving his brother time to process his position.

"Can I go now?" Tielle asks impatiently.

"Soon," answers Jackson. "Gabriel has a report to deliver first." Raising the blue pendant to his lips, he speaks the next question to his brother. "How goes the hunt?"

"We found Marina in Aridel, but a gang of locals attacked before we could speak with her," Gabriel reports. "She was marked in the confrontation. The Huntsman Seeker had her taken to a friend's house in the First Ring to wait for the mark to fade. He's probably been ordered to take her to Bastion, but I don't think he intends to do so."

"Will he be a problem?" asks Jackson.

"I don't know,' says Gabriel. "That depends upon what you intend to do."

"Why do you say that?" Jackson prompts.

"If you try to harm her, he will become your problem," Gabriel promises.

"But I won't be the one going after her," says Jackson.

"I will not kill her for you," Gabriel declares.

"Not even if it came down to Tielle or Marina?" asks Jackson.

"Don't make this about me," says Tielle. "It's about your greed."

Jackson raises a warning finger and waves the rag.

Tielle shakes her head in frustration.

"It's not a fair choice," she mutters.

"Answer the question, dear brother," Jackson demands. "We're both curious."

"I'll destroy the new Keeper's pendant being made for Marina," says Gabriel.

"That's a delaying tactic at best," Jackson notes.

"If she understands the stakes, she'll sign any contract you want," Gabriel insists.

Probably true, but a contract can be broken.

"Try it," Jackson orders. "Make sure the contract has no loopholes and present it to Marina when you can. Impress upon her how many lives rest upon her decision."

"I'll do that," Gabriel promises, "but leave Tielle alone. Please. I can deliver the message when I give our sister the contract."

"Very well," says Jackson. Soon thereafter, he brings the conversation to a close and turns his attention back to Tielle.

She looks up at him expectantly.

"I'm going to release you soon, but first, I want to give you a gift." Jackson indulges in a predatory smile as Tielle flinches. With a snap of his fingers, Jackson conjures a necklace with a silver pendant shaped like a crescent moon. Leaning forward, he fixes the necklace into place. "Keep this on constantly so I can find you. It's enchanted so that if you attempt to remove it or tamper with it, I will know, and the consequences will be suitably severe. Do we have an understanding?"

Chapter 7:
The Visitor

Soaring Oaks, Home of Lady Christa Arrington, City of Aridel
The room Marina wakes up in is larger than Kyle Ricci's entire house. She sits up quickly, startling the woman occupying a comfortable chair placed at the foot of the bed.

"Yer awake! Ya gave me a fright, ya did!" The woman drops her embroidering and rushes around to Marina's right side. "How do ya feel, milady?"

"I feel fine." Marina frowns and looks around the spacious room. Her last memory consists of much darker circumstances. "But what happened? How did I get here?"

"I couldn't tell ya, but if ye agree to wait, I'll go get the mistress," says the servant woman. "Is that agreeable?"

Marina nods, surprised the woman's waiting for her permission.

The woman rushes to the door, streams of long red-gold hair flowing behind her.

"There's a pitcher of water and a glass I readied in case ya get thirsty," she says, pointing to the table set up next to the bed. "I'll have the cook start on a meal for ya. Ye must be starving." She slips out before Marina can reply.

Water sounds good, but mostly, Marina wants answers. Since none await her in the soft, thick blankets covering the bed, she settles for pouring some water into a glass and taking in her surroundings.

The bed sits across from the exit but not directly opposite of it. Two sets of double windows fan out to her left while three are to the right. The left wall has two sets of curtains which are currently open.

One leads to a grooming area, and the other holds many racks of fine clothes. The right wall has several full-length mirrors and a large, ornate vanity set. The dark wall panels balance the light streaming in from the windows, making everything even more impressive. Marina has not seen this much wealth displayed since leaving home.

"Welcome to my home." The greeting comes wrapped in a compassionate female voice that reaches Marina before she even sees the speaker. The lady's blond curls sway gently as she sweeps into the room and approaches the bed. She halts a polite distance away. "My name is Christa Arrington, but please don't hesitate to address me as a friend. The circumstances that brought you here are odd to say the least. I'm sure you have many questions. I've sent for Daniel. As soon as he arrives, we can begin explaining the situation to you. Meanwhile, you have a visitor." Her gray-green eyes sparkle with mirth. She grins and waves toward a window to Marina's right.

A faint scratching noise catches Marina's attention as she spots a red squirrel perched on the windowsill.

"Gabriel!" Delight and fear grip her at the same time. Marina struggles to disentangle herself from the bedding and rise.

Lady Christa gestures for her to stay put.

"I will let him in and give you two some privacy," she says. The lady's refined accent renders the last word differently than Marina's used to, but she finds it charming. "Annie will wait outside the door. When you're finished, please have her fetch me again."

As promised, Lady Christa crosses over to the window and opens it wide enough to admit Gabriel's tiny form.

Marina has never seen him with this exact fur shade before. She admires his attention to detail, but his presence in Aridel alarms her.

"You shouldn't be here!" Marina gets up but forces herself to wait while Gabriel returns to his human form. The desire to embrace him battles with the impulse to reach out and shake him.

The transformation to human form finishes with Gabriel in a crouch. He stands and opens his arms.

Love temporarily conquers concern, prompting Marina to slip into her brother's warm embrace. She's surprised at how tall he's grown. A shot of guilt moves through her for having missed much of his life the last few years. After a long moment, Marina pulls away to study her brother. This sad-eyed young man doesn't fit her memories of the mischievous, joyful child he was once upon a time. His eyes are currently deep blue, but like Jackson, Gabriel inherited the ability to shift the color with very strong emotions.

"Father's ill."

Gabriel's announcement strikes Marina hard.

"With what?" Marina fires the question by reflex. Several questions spring to mind, but she consciously holds them in to give Gabriel time to respond.

"The Healers and Minders don't know," Gabriel says. His features harden with anger. "But I would wager my last breath Jack caused it."

"He wouldn't." The denial sounds as weak as Marina suddenly feels. Painful thoughts about River's Edge try to rise, but she forces herself to focus on the current crisis. "Not yet anyway. Has something changed with Father's will?"

The notion of one day inheriting the full might and wealth behind the Castaloni name always intrigued Marina, but it never tempted her to do anything crazy. She could hardly imagine a world without her parents.

"No, but it might soon," says Gabriel.

"Has he revealed the destruction of my Keeper's pendant yet?" asks Marina. "If not, why not? The contract I signed should give him everything he wants."

"It's not enough unless Father declares it such. You know this, and Jack knows this." Gabriel's voice trembles with frustration. The worry streaming off him goes far deeper than mere concern for their father.

"What aren't you telling me? What more does Jack want from me?" Marina unconsciously holds her breath while Gabriel gathers his thoughts.

Instead of answering, he rapidly cycles through his forms, becoming a beetle then a squirrel and finally a wolf before coming back to human form. He does this twice, a sure sign of his distress and excess energy. The second time he returns to his normal form, Gabriel stays in a kneeling position with his head bowed. His right arm is tucked into his dark robes. Pulling out a thin scroll, he places it on the ground between them.

"He wants you to sign that." Gabriel's voice sounds weary. He keeps his head bowed.

"What is it?" Marina sits on the bed and reaches out with her spirit to sense the scroll. Thankfully, nothing about it feels malevolent.

"A contract and a solemn vow to never step foot in Caramore

again," Gabriel explains.

"What has he threatened this time?" Marina wonders. Although her path has not led her home in several years, the idea that she could always return had been a deep source of comfort.

Could I really accept true exile?

"Tielle. Her sister, Daria. You. Me. Anybody. Everybody." Gabriel recites the list dispassionately as he climbs to his feet, leaving the contract on the floor.

"Tielle?" Marina repeats, rolling the name through her head a few times. "The farmer's daughter?"

"The same," Gabriel confirms. His cheeks redden. "It's my fault. I shouldn't have let Jack know that I care for her!"

Marina agrees but refrains from telling him so.

"Will you sign the contract?" Gabriel keeps his shoulders stiff, as if bracing for bad news.

Heart heavy, Marina shakes her head. Tears sting her eyes as Gabriel's shoulders slump.

"Please," he whispers. "I can't lose her. Not like this."

Getting off the bed, Marina moves close enough to grip her brother's hands.

"I would do it if I believed it would work," she says.

"It worked for River's Edge," Gabriel reminds her.

"Yet here we are again." Marina keeps her voice gentle, but she sees how much the words hurt Gabriel. Her thoughts scramble to find a satisfactory answer. "If we bow this time, there will be another request and another until he finally asks something we cannot give him. We must find another way."

"There is no other way," Gabriel protests. "I thought about returning for her and fleeing, but knowing him, there's a spell or dark enchantment at work."

"Find out for sure," Marina instructs, releasing Gabriel's hands. The problem gets her thoughts rolling on a productive path. "Meanwhile, find some excuse to move her to whatever estate Mother currently resides in. Can you do that?"

Gabriel nods slowly.

"She's been training with Mother in the Conjuring arts."

"Good. She'll be safe with her," Marina reasons. "That should stay Jack's hand for a while."

"Would she be safer with Father?" Gabriel wonders. "He's currently at the Outreach estate, as some of the Minders thought the change would help him.'"

"Maybe, but not if Jack caused his illness," says Marina. Worry sends a chill through her even as hope touches her heart. If Father is in Outreach, perhaps she can go to him. Lack of a Keeper's pendant wouldn't matter in visiting the neutral city. "I will speak with my friends and arrange to visit the Outreach estate."

Is there a way to find out for sure?

"You can't," says Gabriel.

"Why not?" Marina sets aside the problem of figuring out Jack's culpability regarding her father's condition. Maybe Daniel will have some thoughts on the matter, but he's not present to ask anyway.

"I must go, but your Arkonai friends will explain." Gabriel tries to keep a brave face, but his expression speaks volumes about his low spirits.

Before he can escape, Marina hugs him tightly once more.

"I'm sorry you're in this position. Delay Jack's plans as long as you can, and if you find a safe way to tell Father, do so." Pulling his head close, she plants a kiss in Gabriel's thick, dark hair. "Be safe."

"Did you read my letter yet?" asks Gabriel.

Marina shakes her head. Before she can ask about its whereabouts, she spots it on the same table as the untouched glass of water.

"I'll do that soon," she promises.

Accepting her words, Gabriel offers her a slight bow before going to the window and opening it. In another moment, he's gone. Chilly air slips through the gap, so Marina shuts the window. The subtle thunk noise echoes within her heart, feeling very final. Pressing her head to the glass, Marina watches Gabriel scramble down the side of the mansion in his squirrel form.

When he's out of sight, Marina picks up his note and skims it several times. The missive explains the other reason for his presence in Aridel. He has come with Marcus Polani, Gabriella Ricci, and Adaram Serco to bring her back to Caramore so she can fulfill the marriage contract that exists between the Castaloni and Polani families.

Whose side are you on, Gabriel?

Chapter 8:
The Situation

Soaring Oaks, Home of Lady Christa Arrington, City of Aridel

The drawing room Annie left Daniel in is smaller than many of the other rooms in Soaring Oaks. Still, the high ceiling and wide-open spaces make him feel vulnerable. He has to consciously refrain from calling a weapon from the Veil. To distract himself, he taps into one of his less spectacular Gifts and tracks the room's history for the last few days. There's not much to see. Christa spent a few hours reading and letter writing, and Annie and another servant named Hattie cleaned the wood surfaces and changed the flowers.

"You can sit down, you know," says Christa.

"Thank you, but—"

Christa waves off his explanation.

"I know. Huntsmen rarely relax," she says.

"That's not true," Daniel protests half-heartedly. "But I won't relax until I find a way to make this right."

Tilting her head thoughtfully, Christa stares at Daniel.

Heat rises in his face, making him uncomfortable.

"Be honest with me," says Christa. "Who is this Saroth woman, and what is she to you?"

"I've told you," Daniel says quickly. "She's the victim of a misunderstanding."

"What you've told me has been in the presence of the High Council or Jordan," Christa says. "I don't need a report from the Huntsman Seeker. I want the truth from my friend. Do you love her?"

The question sends a rush of conflicting emotions through

Daniel.

"It's not about love!" he declares. "It's about an innocent woman facing the consequences of my mistakes! I signed the contract. I broke it. I should answer for it."

"You are answering for it," Christa assures him. "Remember? That's why we made the arrest. As soon as it's filed, you'll be free and clear."

"I won't do it," Daniel insists.

"Won't do what?" asks Marina. She stands in the doorway with one hand on the door, looking ready to turn and leave.

"Marina!" Daniel fights off an impulse to go to her. He wants to say more, but suddenly can't form words.

"Please, come in," invites Christa, rising graciously. "Be seated. There's much to discuss."

"I have no wish to bring you trouble," says Marina. "Perhaps I should go."

Christa's smile holds both mirth and sadness.

"That would cause us considerably more trouble," she notes, gesturing again for Marina to enter and sit down.

"What do you mean?" Marina crosses the room and sinks onto the indicated chair.

"How much do you know about the situation we're in?" inquires Christa.

"Which one?" Marina asks, rubbing her forehead. "Rather a lot has gone wrong of late."

"Fair point," Christa admits. She glances at Daniel to see if he wants to take over.

He nods for her to continue.

"Allow me to briefly explain," says Christa. "Daniel accepted a contract to end your life for crimes against the village of River's Edge. He discovered you were helping, not harming, so he broke the contract. This part, you probably know."

Marina slowly nods to confirm Christa's guess.

"What you do not know is that the contract came from someone on the High Council," Christa explains. "They are running an investigation into what happened and will likely clear your name. In the meantime, they've charged us with bringing you to Bastion to await the trial."

"And you disagree with these orders?" Marina's inflection creates a question. She looks between Christa and Daniel.

He imagines her clear blue eyes staring straight into his soul.

"You would never leave," Daniel whispers.

"As I said, someone on the High Council is involved," says Christa. "It could mean nothing more than that somebody let their greed prevail, but—"

"It could also mean somebody is trying to provoke your people," Daniel finishes.

"Provoke how?" Marina asks. "My family is wealthy, but we have no influence over the Tariku League. The Saroth people are isolationist by nature. I doubt they'd care about my fate. At best, you'll get a cautionary tale to warn children to stay inside the walls of Caramore."

"The point is, it's not going to happen," Daniel states firmly. "I'm not letting you become a political plaything for the High Council. We should leave soon."

Christa shoots Daniel an alarmed look, which he tries desperately to ignore.

"Daniel, if the arrest isn't filed, you won't be cleared, and they'll track you anywhere."

The warning sends his thoughts racing.

"We don't have to escape permanently," he muses, thinking aloud. "We only need to delay until her friends can return for her. I can file the notice tomorrow then return for Marina."

"Where will you go while hiding?" Christa demands.

"It's a big world," Daniel says with a shrug.

"Have you forgotten about the mark?" Christa fires the question a second time with her intense green eyes.

"What mark?" asks Marina.

"One of your recent attackers had some Seeker abilities," Daniel explains. Frustration rises inside him as he had forgotten that part. "He marked you before your friends drove them off. If we leave Aridel, they could strike again."

"Who were they? Is Kyle safe?" Marina leaps to her feet, ready to rush out and check on her friend.

"He was well when we left him," Christa reports.

"Would they return to harm him?" Marina's voice wavers with worry.

"I believe you were the target," Christa says gently, "but I have also done what I can to protect him by hiring him to gather herbs for me. The extra income should allow him to move in a ring or two."

"Thank you," says Marina. "I'm sure he'll enjoy that. He can find almost any ingredient you could ever want."

"I believe that. As would anyone who has ever seen his house," Christa comments. "The extra space will also do him good."

The three let the conversation lapse, each disappearing into their own thoughts for a time.

"If running isn't an option, what should I do?" asks Marina, breaking the peaceful moment.

"Stay here," offers Christa. Her expression turns surprised and hopeful. "I can't believe I didn't think of it before."

Daniel immediately follows her logic and explains for Marina's benefit.

"Aridel's First Ring is heavily guarded. We can convince the Council to let us house you here until the trial. It will buy us the time to wait for the mark to fade. Once it's gone, we should have no problem escaping the city. We'll find your friends, and they can get you back to Caramore and well out of the High Council's reach." Despite his best efforts, Daniel's heart soars at finally having a viable answer.

A shake of Marina's head causes the hopeful feeling to disappear.

"I won't run. Not if it endangers either of you." A worry line causes a crease across her forehead. Her gaze becomes distant. "And I don't know if returning home is an option for me."

The pain weighing upon her tone moves something inside Daniel. Circling around the couch, he approaches the chair holding Marina, kneels before her, and picks up both of her hands.

"What happened?" Daniel squeezes her hands, trying not to crush them.

Tears glitter in Marina's eyes. She flicks her gaze between Daniel and Christa.

"You have enough burdens. Are you sure you want to add mine to them?"

"Yes." Daniel has never meant anything more.

He's also gratified to hear Christa echo the sentiment.

"Jackson happened," Marina answers. She looks to Christa and tries to explain further. "He's the one who—"

Christa holds up a hand to cut her off.

"The less I know of that tale, the better," she says. "There's a very small chance the Council will seek testimony from me, but any chance warrants caution."

"He's ... my younger brother," says Marina. "In the eyes of the law, that makes me my father's heir."

"Even as a woman?" Wonder fills Christa's question. She looks wistfully around her. "That would make things infinitely easier."

Daniel had forgotten about Christa's situation. Since her parents' death several years ago, the estate has run largely on its own. Christa has worked closely with her uncle to see that things continue smoothly, but she technically doesn't own any of it. Arkonai law dictates that ownership will be conveyed upon her husband, should she ever marry.

Marina smiles sympathetically.

"Yes, women are allowed to inherit property in Caramore," she confirms, "but our laws are probably even more complicated and random and unfair than Arkonai ones. That is why my brother, Jack, feels he has to take such extreme measures to remove me from consideration."

"What has he done now?" Daniel's anger causes the question to come out with a dangerous edge to it. He releases Marina's hands and rises, clenching his fists at his sides. Futilely, he wishes Jackson were present, so he could deal with the man personally.

Breathing in deeply, Marina brushes some tears away.

"He's threatened to kill me, our other brother, a girl Gabriel cares about, and even that girl's sister," explains Marina. She pauses to gain a better grip on her emotions. Her gaze drills into the floor. "Were it a few months ago, I wouldn't believe him capable of carrying out the threat, but now ... I don't know what to believe."

"What does he want in return for not killing you?" Daniel doesn't bother masking his disgust.

"The contract I read had the usual demands and a few surprises," says Marina. "Aside from accepting exile, he wants me to never marry."

"Why would that matter?" Christa inquires.

"Inheritances aren't secure until one can prove they will carry on the family line," says Marina.

"Could you tell someone?" Daniel asks. "Your parents or the Tariku League?"

"That's the other problem," says Marina with a long sigh. "My father is ill. He is head of the house council, but they can and will overrule him if they think he's making rash decisions. I've been away for years. I don't know how many council members would support me if I said something now. Mother might not even believe me, and Jackson would turn the claim into a reason they should go against my father's wishes."

"Do you even want the inheritance?" Daniel asks.

"I would rather it not fall to Jackson," Marina replies. "There's a strong possibility he caused my father's illness, but true or not, he cannot be allowed to control that many lives."

"That doesn't answer the question," Daniel points out. "Do you want it?"

"Truthfully, running the family affairs never held much appeal for me," Marina admits. "I think Gabriel would be the best candidate, but if I agree to Jack's terms, he'll be the one in charge, not the sensible brother."

Daniel has only seen glimpses of Jackson Castaloni's ambition, but he has no doubt that great wealth and influence in that man's hands would lead to much bigger problems.

"Right then. I'll have Annie fetch us some tea," says Christa. "It looks like we'll be here a while longer. I think I need to hear more about your brothers, Lady Marina."

Chapter 9:
Use Your Enemies

Streets of the Seventh Ring, City of Aridel
You must earn this.

With the statement pressed upon his heart and mind, Jackson conjures a small but sturdy dagger. The weapon comforts him, but every step through this wretched city makes him feel dirty.

Stray dogs wander the streets freely, pulling scraps from areas designated for waste and fighting for territory. Glassy-eyed people sit in doorways and lean against walls. These people won't do. They're too exposed. He must find someone isolated.

I will aid you in this but be quick and clean about the kill.

Used to accepting orders from the Master, Jackson lets his steps wander. As he passes a pair of men speaking in low tones, he senses their attention shift. His sweaty hand nearly drops the dagger, so he adjusts his grip upon the weapon.

The men return to their conversation.

Slowly, Jackson's breathing evens out. He continues his slow trek along the most dangerous paths the Seventh Ring can offer. Bright moonlight creates deep shadows out of the nearby buildings. Finally, Jackson's steps lead him into a short alley behind a row of crumbling community homes crammed against the outer wall of Aridel. If he stretches his arms out right and left he can practically touch both walls.

That one.

At first, Jackson's eyes flit over the still form blending in with the shadows against the wall creating a dead-end. His feet carry him close to the figure. With a gentle murmur, the form shifts, allowing Jackson to see the face of a young boy. Dirt and grime darken the lad's skin, but his fair hair stands out in the semi-darkness.

Jackson's feet stop and refuse to move forward, leaving him lurching. Horror seizes his stomach, making him feel suddenly ill.

Kill him.

Everything in Jackson violently opposes the order. His stomach heaves up its contents, causing a burning sensation in his chest. He coughs and retches for several awful moments. Tears stream down his face, and he leans heavily upon the wall, trying not to step in the mess.

"Can I help ya, sir?" The boy's musical accent gives him an air of innocence.

Before Jackson can reply a hand lands upon his left shoulder. Sharp pain lances through the contact spot, forcing a quick, pained cry from Jackson's lips and raw throat. The scream mingles with a slightly longer one from the child. It feels like a sword has been thrust through his shoulder and down deep into his gut. He falls to his knees, head bowed, and eyes clenched against the pain.

"You are weak." The Dark Man's voice flows from the boy's mouth.

Jackson's head snaps up. He forces himself to look at the figure. Despite everything he's witnessed, the sight leaves him speechless. The lad stands before him with feet shoulder width apart, hands clenched at his sides, and facial features twisted into an expression of pure disgust.

Jackson spits several times to clear some of the disgusting taste out of his mouth. The smell of his recent illness drives him to his feet, but he has only strength enough to stagger over to the wall and lean once more.

"I won't—"

The boy holds up a hand to halt Jackson's protest.

"Peace, my young servant. We will work up to this." The boy shifts his shoulders and studies his hands. He paces a few steps left and right in front of Jackson. "This form is ... adequate, but my hold on it is temporary. You will have to grow stronger."

"Why am I in this city?" Jackson asks. He glances around to avoid looking at the Master's current form. Spotting his dagger, he sends it back into the Veil since he no longer has a need for it.

"Near this location you will find the meeting place of the Arkonai Brotherhood," informs the Dark Man. "We're close enough that I think you may use an illusion spell, but do be conscious of the time. You must be well away before it fades, or they will kill you."

"Why would they believe me?" Jackson inquires.

"Gaining their trust might take some time," admits the Dark Man. "Have patience. They may ask you to prove yourself, but I believe you can persuade them. Your sister's presence is an affront to many of their core beliefs. Trust me."

Still uneasy, Jackson struggles to a standing position. Before the last of his nerve can flee, he conjures the scroll to temporarily alter everything about his appearance. He cannot currently see the new features, but when he tested it in the privacy of Fort Medron, the scroll's illusion gave him blond hair, brown eyes, and thicker facial structures.

"Become the part. Use your enemies," encourages the Dark Man.

"How do I know they won't kill her?" Jackson asks. Part of him wishes they would, as it would save him the trouble later, but his master still believes Marina can cause the rifts between the Arkonai and Saroth to deepen.

"They will try, but leave her fate to me," says the Dark Man. "I will make certain help finds her in time. Now go."

Gentle pressure builds in Jackson's head until he begins walking in the direction his master wishes him to go. With effort, he settles his mind and lets his feet follow the silent impulses. Soon, he stands before a thick wooden door.

Knock firmly and answer the questions.

Jackson does so.

Immediately, the door opens a crack.

"Who travels in the dark of night?" demands a deep male voice. Every word holds a challenge.

"A friend. A brother. A shadow," answers Jackson. Instinct makes him affect the strange Arkonai way of speaking.

"How did you find your way?" The man's second question contains only slightly less hostility than the first.

"The Lady's light. The One's might." Jackson voices the expected response with suitable gravity.

The door swings open.

"Welcome, brother," greets the man. He stands aside and waves for Jackson to enter. "What do you seek of the Brotherhood this evening?"

"I bear important information," says Jackson.

The large man stares at him intently.

"You keep your feelings close," he comments at last. "Very well.

You may approach the council and bear your news. For your sake, I hope they like it."

At a gesture from the doorkeeper, another man steps forward, nods curtly to Jackson, and turns to lead him across the dimly lit room to another door. The inner room they enter is surprisingly spacious. Energy orbs trapped in glass containers provide soft white light.

Jackson's heart beats painfully against his chest. He has never been this close to so many Arkonai. Men shuffle left and right to clear a path through to the center. The murmur of indistinct conversations makes the room seem even more crowded. Two chairs dominate the space on the room's left side. A man occupies the left chair from Jackson's perspective, but the right chair holds a beautiful young woman. She is the only woman in the entire room.

Calm yourself. Present your case quickly.

The woman stands and the room falls silent.

"What do you seek, stranger?" asks the woman.

The question momentarily trips Jackson up, for the man escorting him said nothing aloud to her. The obvious answer shakes him, but he recovers swiftly. The escort must be a Seeker and possess Gifts similar to a Minder.

"Only to gaze a moment upon your beauty, my lady," Jackson says, nearly panicking for having already deviated from his practiced script.

The men around him tense. Nobody reaches for a weapon, but their collective attention settles heavily across Jackson's shoulders.

The woman inclines her head a fraction to acknowledge the compliment.

"I was promised important news," says the lady with an exaggerated frown. "You wouldn't want to disappoint me."

The darker meaning to her second statement causes a new flutter within Jackson.

"As you say," Jackson agrees. "I believe I can solve your problem with the Saroth woman."

"How do you—" begins the man seated near the woman.

"Let him speak," interrupts the woman. Her eyes never leave Jackson. "I'm certain his explanation will include the details of *how* he came by this knowledge."

"Nobody was supposed to know about that," complains the man.

"Failures have a way of compounding." The woman delivers the rebuke without even glancing at the man. "Let us hear him out."

"The men will find her," mutters the man, sinking back into his chair and sulking.

The lady's steady gaze prompts Jackson to speak.

"She never left the city."

The comment causes an uproar as every man voices an opinion. *Silence!*

The thought appears in Jackson's mind like his own thought, but he understands that it comes from the man standing at his side. He briefly wonders how many Gifts are shared between Minders and Seekers, but the task at hand requires his full attention.

"How do you know this?" demands the lady.

"My sources matter less than the truth of their reports," says Jackson. "The Saroth woman is hiding among your elite up in the First Ring."

"That is easy enough to verify." The lady signals the man standing with Jackson.

He bows his head and closes his eyes, appearing to fall into a trance. A second later his eyes snap open.

"Truth," he says.

"You have our attention, stranger," says the lady. "Use it wisely. What do you propose we do about this Saroth woman?"

"Draw her into a trap through her friend," says Jackson.

"It won't work. Kyle Ricci has moved into the Fifth Ring." The announcement comes from the seated man. "We'd have to wait until he leaves the city to ambush him."

"We should kill him," mutters someone behind Jackson. "Prove once and for all his kind should stay east of the Badlands."

A murmur of assent rises.

"He's been hired by Lady Christa Arrington," says the lady as much to the crowd as to Jackson. "The position affords him some unspoken protections."

Jackson shrugs.

"Unfortunate, but not a true problem." He waits until the crowd settles before continuing. "The bait doesn't necessarily have to be genuine. Any man could play the part."

"How?" demands the same man who wanted to kill Kyle. "His skin is as dark as the shadows."

You must leave soon.

The man's stupidity makes Jackson bold, but he keeps a tight hold on his temper.

"I have some ideas about that, but I need to make some preparations. I will return when I can." Jackson turns to leave but finds the way blocked by a wall of Arkonai men.

The one directly in front of him crosses his arms.

"We will look forward to your return." The lady's words cut through the thickening tension.

The men part to let Jackson through.

Chapter 10:
Fire and Fear

Soaring Oaks, Home of Lady Christa Arrington, City of Aridel
Three weeks pass with no new information concerning Marina's father or the Arkonai High Council's wishes. The uncertainty involved in both situations worries her. She longs to visit her father, but with the mark still upon her, both Lady Christa and Daniel Saveron stand firmly against the idea. Technically, as long as one of them accompanies her, the terms of her arrest and detainment still get met, but Marina is loath to place her friends in danger. She owes them much. Both have worked very hard to make sure she's comfortable.

It's an unusual arrangement. Besides being confined to the grounds of the Soaring Oaks estate, Marina wants for nothing. Daniel and Lady Christa split the responsibility of watching over her, and they take their distraction and entertainment duties very seriously. The library offers a nearly endless supply of books and scrolls so Marina can continue her studies. Lady Christa has even begun teaching her to make some additional healing remedies. The stables boast some of the finest horses Marina has had the privilege of riding. The gardens contain many peaceful paths to wander down.

Most days, Marina can successfully ignore that she is still a prisoner, but the reality never strays far from her thoughts. She draws comfort from the knowledge that Kyle Ricci enjoys his new position. He spends many hours in the forests owned by Lady Christa's family, gathering herbs and planting new ones to replace those he harvests. Marina joins him each evening to help sort and dry the new acquisitions.

One evening after the sorting ritual finishes, Marina follows Lady

Christa to one of the hospitality suites at the back of the mansion. They play a few rounds of Challenger, a card game that relies as much upon reading one's opponent as it does luck in drawing favorable cards. It has become Marina's favorite game, though Lady Christa insisted she learn a whole litany of games meant for solo play and entertaining company. If a game requires three or four players, Annie or some of the other servants fill in.

The hours pass filled with laughter and friendly competition. Marina and Lady Christa exchange childhood stories, compare various customs and cultural differences between the Arkonai and Saroth, and speak about hopes and dreams. The first time they spoke like this, Marina found it painful to dwell on the past, but Lady Christa's good humor and gentle spirit have done much to help her heal from recent events.

Midway through an idle musing about what it would have been like to have a sister like Lady Christa, Marina spots Tegan, the stable boy, standing in the threshold, waiting for permission to enter. He knocks tentatively on the frame. Since Marina is facing him, she catches Lady Christa's eye and nods toward the door.

"You have a message," Marina says, spotting the black arrow clutched in the boy's hands. The colored arrow system first baffled her, but she has come to appreciate its ease and efficiency. It suits the city's tiered layout perfectly. She can't remember what black means, but Tegan looks nervous.

Rising gracefully from her chair, Lady Christa waves the boy inside and crosses the room to meet him.

"Good evening, Tegan. What do you have for me?" She holds out her hand for the arrow.

"A message, my lady," announces the breathless boy. "Black arrow." He races across the room and presents the arrow to his mistress.

Lady Christa frowns down at the crudely painted arrow with black feather fletching. A narrow scroll has been fixed to the arrow's center and sealed with red wax.

"What does it mean?" Marina asks, wishing she remembered the color code. She rises and joins Lady Christa and the stable boy.

"Nothing good," Lady Christa mutters. Picking up on Marina's confusion, she continues, "Beige or brown arrows are used for most messages. Red is saved for emergencies. Black means a warning or a threat."

They lock gazes.

Unease grips Marina.

The concern etched in Lady Christa's expression says she feels much the same. With trembling fingers, the lady breaks the seal and unfurls the scroll. She skims the message and lets it curl up again, but not before Marina sees the bold letters.

Come to Alkanon Square tonight or the other Saroth dies.

Marina knows of only one other Saroth in Aridel.

Kyle.

"May I see it?" Marina needs to see the message again.

Lady Christa clutches the arrow to her chest and shakes her heads. Slowly, the shock shifts to anger. Her pale cheeks flush and her eyes harden.

"It's a cruel trick. Don't believe it," says Lady Christa.

Carefully, Marina pulls the arrow free from the lady's grasp and rereads the message three times. Each reading chills her further. She must go to Kyle. Looking to Lady Christa, she suddenly has a hundred things to say and no words. Dropping the arrow, Marina sprints out of the room and weaves her way through several short hallways and large rooms until she reaches the front door.

"Marina, wait!" calls Lady Christa.

After fumbling with the door latch, Marina exits and stops suddenly. Her eyes settle on Alkanon Square. Despite the distance, one can easily see a large crowd gathered in front of the Fountain of Beauty. Before she can take another step, Lady Christa catches her left arm.

"It's a trap," she says quickly. "Whoever they are, they know you're safe here. They can't touch you within these walls." Her hand slides down Marina's arm to her wrist. Bright moonlight shines off unshed tears in her eyes.

"I have to go anyway," Marina declares.

"Please don't," says Christa. "They'll kill you both. You're safe here."

"I am, but Kyle's not and he's my friend." Anger hardens Marina's tone, but it's not directed at Lady Christa. "What if it were Daniel? Would you help him?"

Marina sees the questions strike the lady like twin arrows. She regrets causing her friend pain, but she also needs her to understand. Sensing she's won the debate, Marina smiles sadly.

"Will I have to fight my way free?" Her heart sinks at the possibility, and she honestly doesn't know if she can bring herself to lay a hand on her friend, even to save Kyle.

Lady Christa shakes her head slowly.

"I won't stop you, but I am going with you."

Marina shakes her head.

"Find Daniel first. Tell him what happened. Then come," she instructs. Pulling the woman into a tight hug, Marina lets the embrace express some of what she can't articulate. "Thank you for everything. You are a true friend."

When the embrace ends, Marina sees Lady Christa's stubborn and determined express on.

"Tegan, please fetch Starlight for me," says the lady. "We're going together." Lady Christa winces, directing the comment to Marina. "And I'm probably helping you get yourself killed."

Marina wants to comfort her but doesn't know how. They spend the short wait shivering as cold wind takes random stabs at them.

The stable boy returns with a beautiful white horse already saddled and ready to go. Starlight must be the horse on standby tonight. Shadow Oaks always keeps at least one horse ready to ride. Tegan helps Marina into a heavy travel cloak, and then does the same for Lady Christa. Next, he holds the reins while Lady Christa helps Marina up into the saddle and climbs up behind her.

"Get a message to Huntsman Seeker Daniel Saveron," Lady Christa instructs Tegan as she accepts the reins from the boy. "Tell him about the arrow and inform him we're going to Alkanon Square. He should follow as quickly as possible."

Lady Christa turns the horse toward the front gate where two servants are clearing the way for them.

The ride down several city levels passes tensely. Lady Christa steers the horse cautiously on the steeper inclines and makes up ground when the land flattens out. Marina fervently wishes for a specter to magically appear and whisk her down to the destination.

When they arrive in Alkanon Square, the torch-bearing crowd parts to let them through and closes ranks behind them as they pass. Dread pounds through Marina's heart with each of Starlight's clattering footfalls. They're forced to slow the horse to a walk. Marina longs to drive the horse straight through the crowd and keep on going, but she's not in control.

The crowd stares at them. Hostility thickens the cool night air.

Marina shivers with more than cold when Lady Christa halts the horse and hops down. The distance to the ground looks impossibly far, but with the lady's help, Marina's feet soon find the smooth even stones.

A low, makeshift platform has been erected in front of the large fountain. It has a single, sturdy beam running up through the center. A hooded man has been tied to the beam. Scraps of hay and wood have been piled up under his feet.

Fixing her attention on the man, Marina studies him. Relief and fear seize her simultaneously.

It's not Kyle.

This man is shorter and thinner than her friend. When he looks up, the hood shifts enough for her to see his pale skin.

"It's not him," Marina whispers to Lady Christa.

One of the men carrying a torch separates from the crowd near the back of the platform. He too wears a hood, but that's not unusual. Most of the crowd wears thick winter cloaks. The air is not especially cold for this time of year, but the wind can pick up at a second's notice, slicing through most clothing.

"Forgive the deception, but you've got the whole city curious." The man's voice is cool and full of malice. He paces in front of the crowd. Throwing back his hood, he points the torch at them. The move reveals a row of tiny throwing daggers attached to his belt. "Come Saroth. Don't be shy. Show us some magic." The man whips the torch back and forth as if holding them at bay. Sparks fly out and land on the stones at his feet.

"What's going on, Garok?" Lady Christa calls.

"Go home, Christa," says Garok. "This doesn't concern you."

"The Guild may disagree." Lady Christa's tone is civil but icy. She steps in front of Marina. "This Saroth woman is in my custody, and therefore, under my protection, huntsman."

Huntsman Garok glares at her contemptuously, but then, his lips form a hard, cruel smile.

"Don't you know the Saroth are dangerous, my lady?" He spins to face a different section of the crowd and shouts to be heard. Another few sparks leap from the torch and land on the platform. "If we're not careful, they'll infest our cities and steal bread from our children. They'll raise the dead and destroy our wheat fields. They'll—"

"If you're not careful with that torch, you'll light that man on fire," Marina says, interrupting Garok's ridiculous speech.

"That's right. Cut me loose," says the man tied to the pole.

"In due time," Huntsman Garok assures the false prisoner. "But we've gathered a crowd for a show, and we ought to give it to them first."

"Let's go," urges Lady Christa, turning to face Marina. "There's nothing to see here."

"You may go," Garok say, "but she stays until we're impressed."

"What do you think I can do?" Marina asks. With effort, she keeps her voice calm, out she's tired of having people fear her simply because she's Saroth.

"Don't even talk to him," says Lady Christa.

"Saroth study the dark arts. Show us something scary."

Several people in the crowd shout approval and call for Marina to answer Garok's challenge.

Before she can respond, a powerful gust of wind carries sparks from several torches onto the pile of kindling at the false prisoner's feet. That would have been the end of it, but a weaker gust of wind fans the flames.

Marina feels the flames flare to life. An echo of the heat spreads throughout her chest.

The man screams in pain and terror.

"Help him!" Marina cries, rushing forward.

But nobody else moves. The crowd stares at the rising flames, transfixed.

Plucking a throwing dagger from Garok's waist, Marina clambers up onto the platform and frantically cuts at the ropes binding the man. The ones around his ankles snap easily, but the ones around his waist and hands require some effort. When the last one yields, the man falls heavily upon Marina, coughing from the smoke. She staggers under his weight, but soon, a dozen pairs of hands pull the man to safety.

Her travel cloak starts to smolder, so she loosens the ties and casts it off.

Now that the danger to the man has passed, Marina focuses on the fire itself. Reaching for the nearest flame, she stretches deep into her spirit and wills the flame to dim. Not knowing what else to do with it, she draws the fire toward her body and fashions it into a small, bright ball. The energy continues to build as she drains the rest of the flames from the would-be bonfire and three of the nearby torches.

As her energy weakens, Marina feels the fireball's instability grow. If she loses control now, it could explode and kill dozens of people. With a desperate cry, Marina rolls onto her back and channels her remaining energy into casting the fireball up into the night sky. It rises above the wooden beam next to her and keeps going upward. When it's well above the rooftops, Marina spreads her arms wide and releases the energy, willing it to dissipate quickly.

The resulting explosion sends streaks of white fire and ash in every direction.

Stunned silence claims the crowd.

Relieved, Marina rests on the platform, completely spent.

The next thing she's aware of is Lady Christa pulling her half onto her lap. Several tears fall onto Marina's face. Her body shakes with her friend's quiet sobs. Marina wants to sit up and assure Lady Christa that she'll be fine, but she lacks the energy to even lift her head. Closing her eyes, she tries to rally her strength.

"You should look away, Lady Christa," says Huntsman Garok.

Marina forces her eyes open and finds the huntsman kneeling over her, dagger in hand. She's not certain where he intends to stick the blade, but there's very little she can do to defend herself anyway.

"Don't do this. Don't do this." The quiet chant comes from Lady Christa.

"She saved my life. Let her be," says the recently liberated man.

"She's dangerous!" Garok's blade now rests upon Marina's chest. He swivels his head and raises his voice. "Imagine what she could do to this whole city with that kind of power over fire!"

Murmurs turn to rumbles as the crowd debates her fate.

"That's enough!" The new voice rings with authority. "Everybody go home."

Marina turns her head and watches the crowd part to let a man surrounded by four huntsmen through. Another dozen huntsmen spread throughout the crowd and peer down from nearby rooftops. The number of men he commands tells her he's important, but it's not until she feels Lady Christa relax that Marina identifies him. This must be Supreme Huntmaster Ashton Cassel, her friend's uncle. Marina has heard much about him but never laid eyes upon the man.

Garok removes his blade but stays within striking distance.

"This woman performed a feat of black magic the likes of which I've never seen. I have a hundred witnesses," says Garok. "Let me kill her."

Several people start to add their opinions, but the newcomer raises his hands.

"I saw it," assures the Supreme Huntmaster. He walks up to the platform's edge. "But we must learn more before rendering any judgments."

"She's not a threat, uncle," Lady Christa says. "She saved a man's life tonight. Please, let us return to Shadow Oaks."

The crowd boils with opposing opinions.

The Supreme Huntmaster stays silent while considering his options.

Marina sees both compassion and calculated cunning etched in his features. The Supreme Huntmaster might not have jurisdiction within the city, but whatever he says will stand. He could have her escorted back to Shadow Oaks, removed from the city, or even executed. As a Saroth, she has no protections under Arkonai law.

"Take her into custody," he orders at last.

Marina blinks at the man, hoping she'd misheard him.

"No! Uncle, please. She's—" Lady Christa protests.

"This is for her safety, my dear," says the Supreme Huntmaster.

Marina rallies her strength and tries to sit up, but Lady Christa tightens her embrace and whispers directly into her ear.

"I'm so sorry it's come to this, Marina. Please don't fight the huntsmen. They'll take you to the Northgate Prison shortly. I'll visit as soon as I can. I promise. I'll let Daniel know too. We'll think of something."

Chapter 11:
Harsh Reality

Northgate Prison, City of Aridel

"Where is she?" Daniel's question stabs outward with considerable force. Anger and worry mingle in him so strongly that he can barely think straight.

Rising from a bench where she'd obviously been waiting for him, Christa Arrington steps into his path.

"Daniel, please calm down." Christa keeps both hands in front of her body in case she needs to physically hold him back. "She's here, and she's safe."

"For now," adds a deep male voice. "But we need to discuss these matters in private."

Daniel bristles and twists his body to face the newcomer.

"Release her to me," Daniel demands. He tries and utterly fails to make it a respectful request.

"Watch your tone," says Supreme Huntmaster Ashton Cassel. "I could—"

"He's only worried, uncle." Christa shifts position to stand partly between the two men. "We both are. This isn't right."

"We are not discussing this in public," declares the Supreme Huntmaster. "Christa, go home. There's nothing more you can do, and I don't want you involved beyond this point."

"I'm already involved," says Christa.

"She stays," Daniel states almost at the same time.

The Supreme Huntmaster rubs his face wearily.

"Fine. Come into my office," he says. Turning, he leads them to the chambers set aside for him and any other visiting huntsmen. He circles the desk but doesn't sit down. "Sit if you like."

"The Council granted us custody of Marina Castaloni until the investigation completes," Daniel points out as soon as the door shuts behind them. "There's no reason to keep her in prison."

"If I hadn't intervened, she might be dead from that mob," says the Supreme Huntmaster.

Daniel clenches his teeth to keep from calling the man on the lie. Pain moves through his jaw.

"What happened?" The two-word question carries the essence of Daniel's contempt. He moves his hard gaze from the Supreme Huntmaster to Christa.

"We were drawn out to Alkanon Square by a black arrow containing a lie," Christa explains. "The wind caused a fire to break out, and Marina … did something to stop it."

"Something magical," adds the Supreme Huntmaster. He holds up a hand to prevent a response from Daniel. "Right or wrong, that put the crowd into a frenzy, so I took the Saroth girl into protective custody."

"Thank you." Daniel strives to see the situation from the man's point of view. "But that doesn't explain why she remains in prison."

"The incident has made the Council reconsider the previous arrangement." The Supreme Huntmaster directs the statement to Daniel before moving his attention to Christa. "There's not enough security at Soaring Oaks and letting her stay there puts you in danger. I won't have it."

"What if Daniel stayed with us?" asks Christa. "There's plenty of room."

"It's not proper," answers the Supreme Huntmaster. "And anyway, he has duties to fulfill."

"I don't have any current contracts," Daniel argues.

"You will soon," promises the Supreme Huntmaster. Amusement brings a faint smile to his face. "The Council is willing to let you advocate for the Saroth girl."

The statement lifts Daniel's spirits, but he knows enough to expect a catch.

"Under what conditions?" he asks carefully.

Reaching into the desk, the Supreme Huntmaster pulls out a scroll and tosses it to Daniel.

The terms and conditions of the contract flood Daniel's mind.

As promised, the Council offers to let him represent Marina in legal dealings concerning the Arkonai Hunting Guild. In return, they demand regular reports on everything he can learn about the Saroth during his conversations with her.

The Supreme Huntmaster glances at Christa and opens his mouth to send her away.

"If it concerns Marina, he's going to tell me anyway, uncle," says Christa. "You might as well explain to us both."

To emphasize the point, Daniel passes the enchanted contract to his friend.

The Supreme Huntmaster chuckles but doesn't respond right away as he considers them.

"I believe you," he says at last. "Be seated. You may not like some of what I have to say." He gestures to the two chairs in front of the desk and sinks onto the one behind the desk.

Fighting off unease, Daniel politely guides Christa to the right chair before sitting down on the left one.

"I don't like any of this," Daniel notes. "I won't spy for you."

"Before you refuse, consider the alternatives," suggests the Supreme Huntmaster. "You seem to care for this young woman, and you are her only hope of a genuine advocate. Any other man I assign the job will merely be a mouthpiece for the Council. Gain her cooperation."

Daniel is surprised by the man's candor, but he wholeheartedly agrees with the sentiments.

"What does the Council hope to learn from her?" asks Christa. "She hasn't seen Caramore in several years, and she's told me her family has little to do with politics."

"The Castaloni name extends far beyond the magical barriers of Caramore," says the Supreme Huntmaster. He shrugs. "Whether the girl understands the power or not, the wealth standing behind her family name makes her a clear target."

The implication ignites a new burning anger within Daniel.

"Do you intend to ransom her like common criminals?" he wonders.

"I do not. No," answers the Supreme Huntmaster. "But you must understand that the Council contains many more voices than my own. The girl's innocence or involvement in the River's Edge tragedy has never been the question. The only thing that matters from the Council's perspective is what use she can be to us."

The words tear deep into Daniel, making him question

everything. From childhood, he had believed the Guild meant adventure and excitement pursuing criminals and returning lost souls to loved ones.

"While she has information, she has our protection," continues the Supreme Huntmaster. "Beyond that point, her fate becomes a question of which group will pay the most for her life. Her presence has angered many people and intrigued many more."

The harsh statements immediately focus Daniel. The anger brings him to his feet.

"This is wrong, and I won't be a part of it!" he shouts.

"You have to," Christa counters quietly. Her expression mixes pain, anger, and desperation. "Uncle Ash is right. Nobody else will fight for her."

"What am I even fighting?" asks Daniel. "We should free her and escort her to a neutral city or back to Caramore or wherever she wants to go. She's done nothing wrong."

"You have to prove that to every Council member," says the Supreme Huntmaster.

Christa shakes her head sadly.

"You don't mean that," she says with a weary sigh. Turning to Daniel, she continues, "He really means you have to find out what each Council member wants in exchange for voting to free Marina and broker enough deals to win the case."

"Why don't you get started on that, my dear?" suggests the Supreme Huntmaster to Christa. "They already know you and will likely be candid about their desires. You can fill Daniel in on the details later. We have some other matters to discuss, and then, we'll pay a short visit to the young Saroth."

Part of Daniel wants to stop Christa from leaving, but the Supreme Huntmaster's plan has merit.

Both men rise respectfully as Christa reluctantly gets up, hands Daniel the contract, and takes her leave of them. Once alone, they stare across the desk, each trying to gauge the other.

"I like you, Daniel," says the Supreme Huntmaster, waving for him to sit again. "I think you have a level head and a heart that desires justice."

"Then you'll understand why I have a problem with using an innocent woman this way." Frustration bleeds through Daniel's statement, but he obediently sinks onto the chair again.

"The world is a complicated place," notes the Supreme Huntmaster, also sitting. "The Saroth withdrew from the majority of the continent centuries ago. The few who have ventured beyond their borders are mavericks and idealists. In truth, we don't know much about them anymore. We could use this opportunity to educate our people as well as ourselves."

The Supreme Huntmaster's speech mollifies Daniel slightly, but he suspects the man is merely spouting things he wishes to hear.

"I know what the contract says, but I want you to concentrate your efforts on the Saroth woman," says the Supreme Huntmaster. "Christa and I can handle the Council politics. The girl trusts you. Get her to open up and share information about her people."

"She won't betray them," says Daniel.

"What's to betray?" the Supreme Huntmaster wonders innocently. "We are not at war. Make it an information exchange if you like. Tell her how Arkonai society works."

By this time, Daniel's anger has subsided enough to allow him to read between the Supreme Huntmaster's careful words. The Arkonai and Saroth are not at war yet, and the lack of information fuels a general mistrust of each other. This might actually be an opportunity to discover some common ground and nurture the tentative peace that exists.

"I'll accept the contract with a few modifications," Daniel announces.

"What manner of modifications?" asks the Supreme Huntmaster.

"Provisions for Marina's protection for one," Daniel answers.

Closing his eyes, he makes the changes before handing the contract to the Supreme Huntmaster for approval. They go back and forth a few times making slight adjustments before both sides are satisfied with the final contract. Finally, the Supreme Huntmaster plucks a quill from the inkwell and hands it to Daniel who spreads the contract on the desk.

Daniel carefully signs the contract, hoping good will come of it.

"Will that be all?" Daniel asks. He fully expects to be dismissed.

"You could be Supreme Huntmaster someday," comments the Guild leader. "Would you like that?"

A few weeks ago, Daniel would have been flattered by the attention, but his eyes have been opened to a much harsher reality.

"I don't know, sir," he answers honestly.

"Think about it," encourages the Supreme Huntmaster. "I won't be around forever, and Christa will need a good man to marry if something happens to me."

Daniel's gaze sharpens. He had forgotten the rules for replacing the Supreme Huntmaster. Ordinarily, if the office suddenly becomes vacant, the Supreme Huntmaster's son would assume the position until a new one can be elected. However, in cases where the current man has no offspring, succession flows through his nearest living relative.

Christa.

Since Christa Arrington does not belong to the Arkonai Hunting Guild and the office of the Supreme Huntmaster has never been occupied by a woman, the position would go to her husband. Since she has none, the Council could select from its own ranks for an interim Supreme Huntmaster, or if they deadlock, they could allow her to choose by engagement.

"Has something happened?" Daniel inquires, trying to stem the tide of disturbing thoughts.

The Supreme Huntmaster shakes his head.

"Nothing out of the ordinary," he says. "But if you can prove yourself with this Saroth situation, I believe it will go a long way in impressing the Council. You have already impressed my niece." The Supreme Huntmaster waves dismissively as if to brush away the current conversation thread. "No decisions must be made now. These are considerations for the future."

Chapter 12:
Spirit Summoner

Combat Arena, Fort Medron

"Will they suffer?" Jackson wonders.

As he watches, one of the three prisoners futilely tugs at the chains fixing him to the arena pit's circular stone walls. Jackson idly wonders how much longer Dawtan Prison will be a viable source of prisoners. His contact inside the prison said his superiors were starting to ask questions. That's why these men had been recently paroled instead of currently serving their time. Thoughts of the battle to subdue them cause a chill to run through Jackson. Letting the Dark Man inhabit his body during the fight had been necessary but highly disturbing.

"That is the wrong question," answers the Dark Man. Today's vessel was once a Bereft teenager who died in a hunting accident near Glazedale. The shallow grave the young man's friends had dug for him would not have preserved the body from scavengers for long. Jackson's intervention allowed the Dark Man's spirit to temporarily bind itself to the fresh corpse. "You should be more concerned with how much you will suffer if you perform the ritual improperly. This isn't like conjuring a loaf of bread."

"What is it like, Master?" Jackson asks, genuinely curious.

"Who's there?" calls a prisoner. "Release us immediately!"

"Best deal with him before I answer that," suggests the Dark Man.

Seeing the wisdom in this, Jackson leans over the side and casts a bolt of lightning at the speaker's feet. The move causes incredible pain to rip through each of Jackson's fingertips, but it has the desired effect.

The prisoner's dusky features pale, and he falls silent.

Jackson frowns down at the faint spot marking the sand where the lightning struck.

"Why is every bolt weaker than the last?" he asks.

"Because you were not given this Gift," replies the Dark Man, moving past Jackson and descending the stairs to the sandy floor. "The transfer spell never finished its work. If you still had Marina's Keeper's pendant you might be able to master the ability, but as it has been destroyed, you will eventually deplete the stolen power."

"Will she regain her abilities?" Jackson demands.

"Doubtful, but even if she does, that is not the current concern." The Dark Man waves to indicate the three prisoners. "Increasing your own powers matters most right now. You are not a Destroyer, don't covet their abilities. You are a Conjurer, a highly skilled one. With my help and guidance, you will be unstoppable."

A surge of pride lifts Jackson's spirits. The Master does not part with compliments lightly. After relishing the feeling for a short time, Jackson follows the Dark Man down into the sandpit. Anticipation builds inside him. Learning has always come easily to him. Still, the amount of time and effort he's already invested into this ritual is staggering.

As his footsteps take him to the arena's center, Jackson studies the three prisoners. The one to his left and the one in front of him glare defiantly. The third man merely looks weary. They still bear bruises from their first encounter with Jackson.

"What do you want with us, Conjurer?" asks the prisoner on the right.

"Ignore them," instructs the Dark Man. "You require neither their approval nor their cooperation. What you need from them will be drawn once the ritual begins."

"Don't I need a body?" Jackson wonders.

The Dark Man shakes his head impatiently.

"You are not merely shuffling spirits this time. You are creating a form from dust and sand and infusing it with a restless spirit. This creature you fashion, this golem, will return to this world from the Darklands angry and confused. It may heed you. It may not. Be prepared for either outcome."

"Don't do this," pleads the man on Jackson's right. "Let the dead stay on their side of the Veil."

"Silence," orders the Dark Man.

"You're going to kill us anyway," says the man growing bolder. He stands up straighter and leans forward against the chains. "I will not die keeping silent."

The features of the Dark Man's borrowed body twist in anger. Moving close to the prisoner, the Dark Man lowers his voice to a sinister whisper.

"You will if you wish to stay dead. Life energy is required for this procedure, but we can make do with two lives if necessary."

Jackson observes the exchange with interest. It's a bluff. They really should be using four life energies, not three, but the threat works, causing the man to sag against the wall.

"Lady, protect us," murmurs the prisoner. He squeezes his eyes shut.

"She cannot help you," hisses the Dark Man. His hand snaps out and closes around the prisoner's throat.

"We should begin," Jackson says, trying to distract his master. The force of his reaction disturbs Jackson. He knows little about the Lady of Light, save that she serves the One.

"How did a servant of the Lady end up in Dawtan?" asks the Dark Man, ignoring Jackson. He loosens his grip enough for the man to answer.

"I … lost my way," says the man. The position of his neck prevents him from looking away from the Dark Man. "Greed led me to kill a man."

The Dark Man releases the prisoner's neck but remains close to him.

"Would you serve me?" inquires the Dark Man.

"I would," declares the man directly in front of Jackson. "How can I serve you, Master?"

"Your life is your service." Stepping back until he stands beside Jackson, the Dark Man stretches his arms out toward the prisoner on the left and the right.

At first, Jackson sees no change, but a second later, the three prisoners cry out in pain and fight the chains holding them.

"Begin your work, Conjurer," orders the Dark Man over the sudden cacophony.

Horror grips Jackson, urging him to flee, but fear roots his feet in place. His mind goes eerily blank. Then, the long hours of study kick in and fill his mind with the required words and movements. He doesn't even know what language the incantation was written in or what changes will be made in him.

The intent is to tune his mind to the spirits beyond the Veil and get them to inhabit physical forms again. Normally, it would be done with a fresh body, but this summoning must be accomplished under the hardest conditions. The first task involves fashioning a body out of sand and mud. Since the arena has plenty of sand, Jackson only needed to haul in a little dirt and water to form mud. The building phase takes him several hours by itself.

The second, more dangerous task requires him to capture a spirit and force it to animate what never had life in it. The work is mentally, physically, and spiritually draining. As warned, some spirits resent being called out of the Darklands. These see Jackson as a threat, so they attack him. The Dark Man channels energy from the prisoners to sustain him during these attacks. The strain drives Jackson to his knees several times, but each time, he pushes through the pain of cramping muscles and the feverish rush of blood through his veins to rise and continue.

By the end, the prisoners are dead, and Jackson barely clings to consciousness. When the last phrase finally passes his lips, he lets his body collapse face-first onto the sand near his creation. He manages to cushion the fall slightly by landing on his arms. His head faces left toward the still figure of a man fashioned from sand.

I failed.

"You did not fail," counters the Dark Man, responding to Jackson's thought. "Rise and see what you have made. Then, kill him and release the spirit." Kneeling over Jackson, he places a hand on the center of his back and transfers the last of the stored vitality.

Anger rises in Jackson as his strength returns. Pushing himself up and around to a sitting position, he frowns at his master.

"Why would I release him?" he demands. "I want to control him."

The sand figure shifts like a man slowly awakening.

"You will release him because you are in no condition to fight him," replies the Dark Man. "To control him, you must make him submit, and you are currently too weak to do so. In time, you will learn to draw the required strength without me." The Dark Man offers Jackson a hand up.

Accepting the help, Jackson rises. His head hurts and his limbs tremble with fatigue. Conjuring a small dagger, he stabs the sand figure in the chest. The figure screeches with rage. Strong hands clamp around Jackson's shoulders and squeeze painfully. The sand man sits up, pulling

Jackson down at the same time. Next instant, the figure collapses back into a pile of sand, leaving Jackson staring down at his half-buried dagger.

"You did well, but you are young and still have much to learn about the powerful side of the Conjuring arts," says the Dark Man. "I must retire this vessel for now. Rest. Tomorrow you must check on your father's health. The situation with your sister is progressing slower than anticipated. The poisoning process must be slowed too, or your father will die before the proper moment."

Chapter 13:
A New Guard

Northgate Prison, City of Aridel

As she does each day, Marina spends the first few minutes looking around her cell. It's surprisingly cozy thanks to the efforts of Daniel, Christa, and their friend, Jordan Lekros. Much like prisons in Caramore, family and friends can greatly improve a prisoner's situation by bringing in fresh food and furnishings. Marina silently thanks the One for their many visits and thoughtful gifts.

Christa had servants bring soft bedding from Shadow Oaks and several decks of cards. She also personally delivered a small inkwell, a new quill, and letter writing parchment. Jordan donated a sturdy wooden chair with intricate carvings over every surface and a small, flat tray that allows her to write letters. The prison authorities insisted on fixing the chair to the floor, so it can't be turned into a weapon. They said nothing about the makeshift desk. Daniel visits often and stays far longer than he needs to in order to fulfill his obligations to the High Council.

After the first few days of lengthy interrogations, the prison officials and the Council largely ignored her. Daniel keeps her informed on where they stand. They sent an envoy to Caramore to determine what the Tariku League's response would be. If they'd asked her, she could have predicted the response would be to not interfere.

At times, worry threatens to drive Marina into despondency, but the support from her friends sustains her. She never expected the length of her stay to exceed a week, but the days quickly became weeks. In another few days, she will finish her third month in prison. Some days, they allow her to walk the halls and a small courtyard with Daniel and a guard, but most days, she spends every waking moment in this tiny cell. It would be peaceful if she couldn't occasionally hear screams from other sections of the prison.

"Morning meal is here," announces a male voice Marina doesn't recognize. He slides a tray under the bars making up the door and tosses a chunk of stale bread onto it. His broad forearm barely fits through the bars. A scar runs down the right side of his neck. Thick brown hair covers his head, but like most Arkonai young men, his face is clean shaven.

"Where is Holt?" Marina wonders, watching the bread roll off the tray.

Christa sends fresh bread, fruit, and pastries for Marina and the guards each morning. The provisions have only reached her twice, and both times, they were delivered by Holt.

"Gone," replies the guard. He tosses a cup of water onto the tray. It too bounces off, spilling its contents across the floor.

Ignoring the attempts to provoke her, Marina climbs out of the bed and selects a clean set of robes from the crate in the corner. She quickly changes by pulling the robes over her head then slipping out of the night dress. Since she only has one, Marina carefully folds the night dress and places it at the foot of the bed.

The guard looks disappointed but watches carefully as she stoops to right the cup, collect the tray, and pick up the bread. She probably won't eat it, but she can't leave it on the floor to attract unwanted visitors either. Finding the bottom speckled with white mold, Marina returns it to the tray and mildly thanks the guard for the delivery.

"You Saroth always think you're better than us," says the guard. His voice is low and full of bitterness. "Hiding behind your fancy magic. Why don't you just spirit yourself away from this place?"

"Because I'm not a Conjurer," Marina replies. "Besides, I'm sure the prison has wards to prevent that kind of magic being used."

"What are you?" asks the guard.

Choosing to misinterpret his meaning, Marina sits on the bed and regards the angry guard. Normally, irritation would fill her, but this time, she feels only pity.

"I am a servant of the One," she says. "I possess a few other titles, but they don't matter much in comparison."

"You will have no title soon," says the guard darkly. Slowly, he slips a heavy key into the lock and swings the door open. "Do you hear that?" The man stops in the doorway and cups his right ear for effect.

"That is the sound of nothing and nobody coming to save you." He plucks a dagger from a sheath on his waist and steps into the cell.

Fear drives Marina to her feet. Reaching down blindly, she picks up the wooden slab meant for writing letters and holds it in front of her.

Laughing, the guard rips it from her hands and shoves her hard. Pain flares from both hands. The back of her legs strike the bed, forcing her to sit again. Before she can recover, he knocks her flat onto the bed. One large palm covers the entire lower half of her face, driving her head into the soft blankets. His other hand holds the dagger's cold blade at her throat.

"Don't worry. I'll make this quick," promises the guard. "The Brotherhood sends its regards."

"You can keep them and your life if you leave right now."

The new male voice belongs to Daniel, but Marina's current position prevents her from seeing anything but the guard looming above her.

"Same offer," replies the guard. "Leave and live."

Marina fights to turn her head so she can breathe. The pressure on her face increases painfully, but the guard shifts his grip slightly to allow for airflow. She draws a slow, shaky breath.

"Let her go, and we have a deal," says Daniel.

"If you interfere, I will kill you both," continues the guard, as if Daniel had never spoken.

The thought of Daniel's death hurts Marina more than her stinging hands or the dagger at her throat. Her hands feebly grip her attacker's arms. She lets her body grow still and closes her eyes, waiting for the next moment to bring death or deliverance.

"She's under the Council's protection," says Daniel. "Even if you exit the prison, the Council will send a dozen huntsmen after you."

"You mistakenly think I want to live," mutters the guard.

His hold on Marina's face slackens enough for her to twist her head right and look at her friend. Daniel stands outside the cell with his bow ready for action. The deadly arrow tip doesn't waver.

Please go. She tries to convey the message with her eyes.

"You family is gone, Roland," Daniel says gently. "Marina had nothing to do with that."

"She's one of them!" cries the guard. "They all deserve to die!"

"This kind of general vengeance is hollow," Daniel presses. "And it could make matters worse. Kelia wouldn't want that."

"Get out of my head!" snaps Roland. Twisting his torso, he flings

80

the dagger at Daniel. With a roar, he leaps from the bed.

Daniel barely has time to knock the dagger aside with his bow before the large man slams into him, driving him hard into the wall. They trade punches evenly and wrestle to gain the advantage. Roland has more height and mass over Daniel, but the huntsman has more experience fighting hand-to-hand.

Captivated by the sight, Marina moves to the open cell door. She stops short of the enchantment covering the doorway. The signal embedded in the silver bracelet fastened to her right wrist will alert every guard in the prison if she leaves the cell. She has also been told it will give her great amounts of pain, but the warden did not elaborate on that point.

At first, it looks like Daniel will emerge the victor, but then, a hard punch catches his jaw, stunning him. Roland scoops up his fallen dagger and moves to end the fight.

Bracing herself, Marina shoves her right hand through the magic barrier. She cries out and collapses as the bracelet clamps tight around her wrist. The burning pain causes her vision to blur with tears. Instinctively, she tucks the wounded arm close to her chest and grips the cell bars for balance. Every few seconds, new waves of agony travel up her arm.

An arrow appears in Roland's chest, then two more. The dagger tumbles from his fingers and lands near Daniel's head.

Several guards rush forward and catch him before he can crush Daniel.

As soon as he's free, Daniel pushes his way into the cell and sits down behind Marina. She's only dimly aware of the many weapons trained on her.

"Move aside so we can subdue the prisoner, sir," orders a young male voice.

"She doesn't need subduing," Daniel mutters. "She's been through enough."

Releasing her grip on the cell bars, Marina leans back into Daniel's embrace and shuts her eyes again. They can argue her fate while she rests.

"She tried ta escape," says another guard with a Bereft accent. "We need ta get her into confinement."

"She didn't try to escape," Daniel argues. "She activated the enchantment to bring the rest of you here so you could deal with him." His rough fingers slide along Marina's arm, stopping at the enchanted bracelet. "Now, get that off her."

"We can't," answers the Bereft guard. "Only Warden Clark or the Healer can turn it off."

"Then go get them!" Daniel orders.

The pain subsides to a tolerable level, letting Marina think again. She grasps Daniel's hand and waits with dread for the bracelet's next round of punishment.

The guards wage a quick debate over who should go and who should stay, but finally, two young guards race off in opposite directions.

"Do you want me to move you to the bed?" Daniel asks.

Marina starts to answer but the burning pain resumes, making her feel like fire ants are trying to gnaw off her hand. Her efforts turn to keeping conscious and not screaming. She can't stop the tears, and she's too tired to be embarrassed by them.

"You can cry," Daniel whispers. He changes positions and settles her partly across his lap. "I'll hold you. I won't leave you. I'm sorry this happened."

"Not your fault," Marina says. "You saved me."

"And you saved me," Daniel reminds her. "Why did you do that?"

Marina's not sure how to answer him, but she's spared the need as the bracelet torments her wrist again. Her hands are slick with sweat, but she clings to Daniel's hand anyway.

"Just a little longer," Daniel encourages. "Once they deal with the enchantment, I'll destroy it. I should never have let them do it in the first place. I'm so sorry."

Marina's heart aches with too many sorrows to list. Her gaze falls upon the dead guard. Daniel must have used his Seeker Gifts to draw out some of Roland's story.

"How long will we do these things to each other?" Marina's question is loud in the silence.

The remaining two guards stare at her stone-faced.

"I don't know, but the One and the Lady willing, we will find a way to stop it." Daniel's statement carries both weariness and determination.

Chapter 14:
Saroth Delegation

Northgate Prison, City of Aridel

"Keep her arm steady," instructs the Healer. "This part is critical."

Following the Healer's directions, Daniel moves into position behind Marina. Crossing her right arm over her left across her chest, he traps the damaged hand between his, holding it steady. The new security bracelet presses into his arm. He argued fiercely against the idea, but the longer he argued, the more time passed before they would let the Healer remove the faulty bracelet. Marina had mercifully passed out from the pain several minutes ago.

The process of deactivating the signal crystals embedded in the bracelet went well, but the metal itself must have been damaged by encountering the field placed across the cell. Instead of releasing Marina's wrist upon deactivation, the bracelet tightened even more. Daniel can barely look at her right hand, which is turning bluer with each passing second.

"Will she be—"

"Young man, the sooner you let me finish, the quicker I can answer that question," says the Healer irritably. "I suggest you look elsewhere while I work. You're already looking ill. If you faint, you won't be of any use to me or this young lady."

To distract himself, Daniel reviews the history of Marina's cell starting with her waking up this morning. He watches Roland deliver the bread and water and sees the short conversation that happened before his arrival. The physical threat to Marina summoned Daniel from his temporary quarters at the Guild's barracks in the Fifth Ring. He tenses at the memory.

A sharp snapping sound pulls him back to the present.

"There. She's free," announces the Healer. "Give me a moment to prepare a suitable healing agent and wrap it. I'll need you to hold her hand out so I can apply the cream."

The Healer quickly mixes a sharp-scented concoction of herbs and green paste. Then he scoops up a generous amount of the cream and gently rubs it on Marina's wounds. Finally, he wraps the wrist and arm tightly with clean strips of linen.

"Keep this clean and dry and make sure she stays rested," says the Healer.

"Will she be able to use the hand again?" Daniel wonders, knowing Marina will want that information.

"Given the stubborn head on her shoulders, likely," replies the Healer. The man frowns at Daniel. "I hope you deserve such devotion."

Daniel gives the man a questioning look.

"Wake up, boy," grumbles the Healer. "She wouldn't have risked losing a hand if you didn't mean something to her. Now, get that stupid grin off your face. I may not care what foolishness young hearts get up to, but there are thousands more who would kill you for the thought."

The statement sobers Daniel.

Clearing his throat, the Healer continues, "I shall leave the rest of the cream with you. If you can competently change the wrappings tonight, do so. Otherwise, call me. And call me whenever you run out of the cream."

"Thank you, Master Cordova," says Christa. "But we've inconvenienced you long enough. If you leave a list of ingredients and instructions, I can make it myself."

The sound of the man's name causes Daniel to instinctively collect the rest of his name from his surface thoughts. He's not as proficient at reading thoughts as a Minder would be, but he can glean simple pieces of information on occasion.

"Lady Christa, what a delightful surprise." Emeric Cordova rises to greet her.

Daniel moves to rise as well, but a gesture from Christa stills him.

She exchanges pleasantries with the Healer before letting him out of the cell and dismissing him. Once he leaves, she enters the cell and sits in the chair beside the bed.

"I heard what happened." Christa glances over her right shoulder at the ground outside the cell.

The guards cleaned up well, but Daniel cannot easily forget that a man's life had ended violently in that very spot less than an hour ago.

"Do you want to talk about it?" asks Christa, facing Daniel and Marina again.

"Not really," Daniel answers.

For a time, they sit in silence, but eventually, Daniel's legs start to cramp from being folded beneath him so long. Gently, he lifts Marina enough to be able to climb off the bed. Without comment, Christa helps by steadying her shoulders and easing her down. Pulling up some of the blankets hanging off the side, Christa arranges Marina's wounded arm across her stomach and tucks her in like a small child.

"Christa, we can't keep her safe within the prison," says Daniel.

"Stop talking," Christa murmurs. She makes a show of straightening the blanks around Marina. "We can discuss this later."

Anger spikes inside Daniel's chest. Marina may look peaceful in slumber, but her pain still hangs in the air. Part of him wishes to wake her to see her blue eyes. Her long, dark hair pools around her on the pillow. She's only a few years younger than him, but sleep lends her an innocence that makes her appear far younger. The thought that he can't protect her terrifies him.

"I don't care if they're listening, or if they'll read the conversation later!" he shouts. "They know where I stand."

"They know, and they're currently ignoring it," Christa says softly. "But if you provoke them, they will move her to Bastion where you and I cannot follow. Uncle Ash has threatened this many times."

"Excuse the interruption, Lady Christa, but there's a Saroth delegation demanding to speak with the prisoner," says the guard commander, Tirek Suleron. "The Supreme Huntmaster is away, but he left instructions that such questions should be brought to you. Shall I send them away?"

Christa looks to Daniel for his opinion.

He shrugs. Such delegations come once or twice a week. Usually, they bear small gifts for Marina and the news that nothing has changed with the Tariku League but that the hearts of the Saroth people stand with her. She's not exactly ready to greet visitors, but the travelers deserve to see that Marina's alive before returning to Caramore.

"Let them in, commander," says Christa. "Have you informed the warden yet?"

"He's currently away as well, ma'am," answers Commander Suleron. "Shall I have the guards wait with them?"

"We can manage without them," Christa replies. "Huntsman Seeker Daniel Saveron and I will escort them out when they finish."

Bowing to Christa, the commander retreats.

"Should we wake her?" asks Daniel. "It might do her good to visit with …"

"People not trying to kill her," Christa finishes with a thin smile. "Probably, but let's wait until we see who comes to call first."

A short, painful wait later, two familiar figures stand outside the cell door. Daniel makes introductions for Christa's sake, forgetting that she's had previous dealings with them. There's something different about Marcus Polani and Gabriella Ricci today, but Daniel cannot dwell on the impression.

"We would like to speak with my intended," says Marcus.

The formality and stiffness in his tone puts Daniel on the defensive. The Saroth man's thick wavy black hair hangs across his forehead. Hair covers most of his face, framing his mouth.

"Allow us to wake her for you but know that there may be many witnesses to everything said," Christa warns.

"No, there won't," counters Gabriella. "I will block the Seeker and hold a thought shield in place temporarily, but please, make this a quick exchange."

She stays outside the open cell while Marcus enters.

Christa wakes Marina.

Once conscious, Marina insists on sitting up.

Marcus kneels before Marina and keeps his gaze lowered as he addresses her.

"I know we have not met before, but my name is Marcus Polani. Our houses have formed a marriage contract between us, but it is one I cannot fulfill. My affections belong to another. I humbly come before you today to ask release of the contract. I understand that the breach is mine and will bear the consequences. What can I do to make this right?" Upon uttering the last question, Marcus finally raises his eyes to look at Marina.

"I release you," says Marina, looking relieved.

"You don't want anything?" Marcus asks, stunned.

"I told you she wouldn't," calls Gabriella.

"I want a great many things, but I require nothing of you," answers Marina. "My parents may have some demands to save face, but I will write them on your behalf. In truth, I feel the same. You must already know this since I ignored the summons to come home and meet you. Why seek me out in a prison?"

"I like her," comments Gabriella. "Always have."

The joy radiating from Gabriella makes Daniel focus.

"I take it you and the Minder—" Daniel begins.

"Well done, Seeker," Gabriella praises. "Marcus needs to marry soon so his father can chase ghosts in the Badlands with a clear conscience." She flicks her eyes to Marina. "No offense, but things here could drag on for years."

"I hope not," Marina says.

"Yes! We have some ideas about that too," Gabriella notes. "Oh, Marcus, get up. She's already released you. Tell her the plan."

Marcus stands, but mention of a plan etches a concerned expression on his face. He rests his attention on Christa and Daniel in turn.

"I can feel you wish to free her, so I will trust you," he says. "Gabriella believes we can secure Marina's release by switching them."

"If I take your place, Lady Marina, I can make it seem as if you've never left," Gabriella explains. "You could walk right out the front gates and they'd ignore you completely."

Daniel's heart warms at the possibility, but Marina's next words kill the fledgling hope.

"I appreciate the concern, but won't your plan leave you trapped here in my place?" asks Marina.

"For a time," Gabriella admits. Her eyes brighten with a new thought. "But if Marcus and I marry before the escape, his family will be obligated to ransom me. The Polani name still carries some weight with the Tariku League."

"That might work in Caramore, but things work differently in Aridel," says Daniel. He fervently wishes he could support the plan, but he refuses to trade one innocent life for another. "If you set Marina free, you'd be tried in her place."

"The plan has merit, but it bears much more thought," says Christa. "Let us meet at Soaring Oaks later to go through some details."

Marina opens her mouth to protest, but Gabriella speaks.

"I can share the conversation with you as it unfolds if you like, Lady Marina."

"Very well then," Marina says. "After that discussion, I'd like to talk about a different matter, a more personal one."

"What could be more personal than getting out of prison?" Daniel inquires.

Gabriella flashes Daniel an amused smile.

"If the scan of her surface thoughts speaks truth: saving her family," Gabriella answers.

Marina nods agreement.

Minders can scan surface thoughts?

Each new thing Daniel learns about Minders fascinates him. He always knew some Seekers gain that ability. At times, he can even do so himself, but he knows little about Minder abilities.

What else are they capable of?

Chapter 15:
A New Deal

Private Gardens, Castaloni Estate, City of Outreach

Corabelle Castaloni rises from the fountain's edge as a servant ushers her young guest into the courtyard clearing. Marcus carries himself well, showing little of the nervousness he must be feeling. She too would be uneasy if she were marching into a rival estate about to break a contract. Her informants might not be elite Minders, but they're good enough to keep her up to date on the household affairs. In this case, she has the most reliable source: her son, Gabriel. Her youngest child couldn't keep a secret from her if his life depended upon it. He tries, but his expressions always reveal when something weighs upon him. He's worn a haunted look for quite some time.

Since Marina left, she silently admits.

Forcibly, Corabelle focuses on the current situation. She hasn't decided how she wishes to play the knowledge cards she possesses, but as Marcus approaches, she decides to speak plainly. The Polani heir never struck her as a politically savvy man. In that sense, he's very much his father's son. In fact, the last Polani man to truly embrace his position on the Tariku League was Marcus's great-grandfather, Orak.

"Greetings, Lady Corabelle." Marcus dips his head in a polite bow. "I had hoped to see your husband today, but the servant said he is currently resting and suggested I speak with you."

"That is correct," says Corabelle. "I am handling household matters in his stead until he recovers. That is why we are in the south. What did you wish to discuss with him?"

Marcus hesitates. He lowers his head and studies the ground as if it holds answers for him.

The move reminds Corabelle of Gabriel as a small child come to confess something to her. Compassion prompts her to ease his mind.

"Gabriel told me of recent developments," says Corabelle. "He even said you saw my daughter in the Arkonai prison. How is she?" Despite her best efforts to remain aloof, Corabelle's heart thuds painfully within her at the thought of her firstborn being locked away far from home.

"Very well for the circumstances," Marcus replies. "They've kept her separate from the rest of the prison population. The cell is small but clean, and she has friends seeing to her needs each day."

Blinking away tears, Corabelle nods tightly and waves for Marcus to continue his explanation.

"I went to see her for several reasons," says Marcus. "I wanted to secure her release from the marriage contract and inform her of the plans to help her escape."

"What plans?" asks Corabelle. She knew about the contract part, but nobody had mentioned any escape plans to her. Hope and fear leave her stomach lurching.

"They are not finalized yet, but we are working closely with Marina's Arkonai friends to secure her release," Marcus explains.

"Has the Tarika League given up on her?" Corabelle asks. She knows definitively that they never entertained the notion of bargaining for Marina's life, but she wants to know how honest Marcus will be with her as that will dictate how harshly she deals with him.

He avoids her gaze.

"They ... decided to not intervene," he answers carefully. Determination enters his expression as he lifts his eyes to hers again. "But I said I would find Marina, and I mean to keep my word. I cannot guarantee where she will go once free, but if it lies in my power, I will break her out of that prison."

"May I assume you obtained Marina's release of the marriage contract?" asks Corabelle, ignoring his promise for the moment.

"I did," Marcus confirms, brightening a little. "She said she wanted nothing from me, but that you—her parents—might make some demands. That is what I wished to discuss with your husband."

"I believe we can help each other." Corabelle conjures a sturdy wicker chair for Marcus. "Would you like any refreshments?"

He declines with a brief shake of his head but perches on the chair.

"We both understand that the alternate contract your parents proposed between Gabriel and your sister is doomed from the start," notes Corabelle, resuming her seat on the fountain's edge. "Marina has shown little interest in fulfilling the original contract, as demonstrated by her quick agreement to its demise, but you brought up the breech first."

Marcus visibly braces for her next words.

Corabelle makes a placating gesture.

"I have no wish to drag this out any longer than necessary," she assures the young man. "We could take these matters before both house councils and witness the ugly legal battle that ensues, or we can reach an agreement on our own."

"What do you want?" Marcus asks.

Chuckling at his bluntness, Corabelle conjures a wooden table with a pitcher of water and two clear glasses.

"You have no interest in Council affairs," Corabelle states, pouring Marcus some water before filling the second glass for herself. "I do," she adds, bidding Marcus to drink. She takes a few sips to prove that the water is free of poison. Setting the water glass down, she watches beads of sweat form on the sides.

"You want to join the Tariku League?" Marcus's question contains more curiosity than consternation. "I suppose I could sponsor you the next time there is an opening."

"I had more in mind to create an opening," says Corabelle, waiting for Marcus to catch her meaning. After several beats pass with little to no reaction, she explains further. "The position your father holds is purely ceremonial. He cares nothing for it and would gladly relinquish it to you upon request."

"And you wish me to turn it over to you," Marcus concludes. His expression turns wary.

"In the interest of bettering both our houses, yes," says Corabelle. Sensing the moment has arrived, she creates a small opening in the Veil and summons the contract she had her advisers prepare. "In this contract, you will find most of the terms and conditions from the previous one, with amended parts involving whom you'll marry, of course." Holding out the scroll, she waits for Marcus to take it.

Having little choice, he does so. A grin destroys his thoughtful frown, letting Corabelle know when he reaches the marriage clause.

"My son tells me you've grown close with Gabriella Ricci," says Corabelle. "Her mother is alive, but her father is not. She currently lives with her mother and stepfather on lands bearing the Castaloni name.

91

She has reached the age of majority, and I will not force her to do anything against her will. However, if she convinces her mother to terminate parental rights, we will formally adopt her—in name only—with the understanding that she marries you soon thereafter."

"Would her mother agree to this?" Marcus wonders.

"Further down the contract, you will find the provisions I included to aid her request," says Corabelle. "In addition to liberating the land they work, I have included a stipend to aid with any social transitions. Her younger sister works at the estate in Dominance. She will be free to continue that service or enroll in any training program she qualifies for. I believe knowing this, her mother will agree."

"You could do this without her mother's consent," Marcus points out. "Is it not true that every indentured servant belongs to the house?"

"You have known Gabriella for a short while," Corabelle says. "I watched her grow up In your opinion, how do you believe she would react to being forced into such a thing?"

"Not well, my lady," answers Marcus. He lets the scroll curl up again. "Still, those are very generous terms. It makes me wonder why you are doing this."

"It is as much self-preservation as generosity," replies Corabelle. "My husband may very well be dying, and my daughter, his heir, is not currently present. Should my husband pass without these matters being settled, they may never conclude, and we would both miss an opportunity."

Marcus's expression says he wishes to know more but is too polite to pry.

Corabelle needs no special powers to see into the future. Jackson will challenge Antonio's will and inadvertently throw most of their holdings into chaos. As much as she loves her elder son, Corabelle knows he has entirely the wrong disposition to run the businesses well. He cares only for the money and the power and nothing for the work involved in keeping the businesses profitable.

"I am trading wealth I can afford for influence I could not otherwise obtain," says Corabelle, surprised she has to spell things out for the young man. "And I am asking you to use your family's connections on my behalf in exchange for the money your holdings desperately need to survive."

"You have given me much to consider," says Marcus.

Corabelle raises a hand to stop the rest of his speech.

"I know you have many people to consult." She lets a genuine smile form. "Certainly, Gabriella awaits news of our conversation, if she's not already heard. The privacy wards around this estate are not what they once were. I only ask that you reach a decision quickly."

"You will have my answer by tomorrow," Marcus promises. Getting up, he offers her another bow. "Thank you."

As she watches the young man retreat, Corabelle does not envy him the difficulty of his decision. Although on parchment the offer makes perfect sense, it will not be easy to convince his mother to accept it. Corabelle wonders if he even told her about Gabriella.

Elena Polani hails from the upper echelons of society. She will not enjoy knowing that her eldest child intends to marry a lowborn woman. As someone who married up, Corabelle possesses a different perspective, one that allows her to accept Gabriel's poorly concealed courtship of Tielle Toscano.

He's not the child who worries her the most. That distinction gets split evenly between Jackson and Marina. Corabelle doesn't know what initially sparked the hostility between them, but Jackson's unbridled greed has only made it worse.

If he could only see that the titles matter less than the reality.

Marina would gladly leave control of everyday affairs to either brother. She would probably even donate her portion of profits to feed homeless children in some dirty village nobody has ever heard of. Clearly, she too lacks the sense to successfully steer the family affairs. The difference is that Marina would admit such and delegate well. Most of the managers know their businesses well enough anyway.

Jackson will not delegate or admit when he's wrong.

Though it tears at her heart to have to choose between her children, Corabelle decides to do everything possible to see that Antonio's current will is honored.

If only you were less like your father, Marina. Your good heart is going to lead you to grief.

Chapter 16:
Letters from Northgate Prison

Marina's Cell, Northgate Prison, City of Aridel

During the course of Marina's recovery, Daniel insists on being her scribe as she answers the many scrolls and missives from people near and far. If she didn't crave company so much, she might question the amount of time he spends at the prison, despite assurances that her security has been increased.

At first, Marina wasn't sure how to answer those reaching out to her with unsolicited support or condemnation, but the activity eases the boredom. She has come to enjoy the afternoons dictating letters to Daniel. His handwriting is smooth and beautiful. He would read the letters anyway, as will many others before they leave the prison, so there's no use trying to conceal anything. At times, they go back and forth on a section for hours, trying to find the perfect wording, but mostly, he says little while she unburdens her soul to friends and strangers.

Today's letters will be different.

Daria Toscano arrived the previous evening, bearing the happy news of Gabriella's rise in station and pending marriage to Marcus Polani. She also brought a letter from Marina's mother, which explains the arrangement in more detail. The servant stayed overnight in the prison to await Marina's answering letters.

***

Dear Mama,

I know we have had our differences, but thank you for letting me know of these events. I have read your letter many times. If I close my eyes, I can hear your voice speaking to me. It makes me smile and miss home very deeply.

Gabriella has visited several times over the last week, and we are fast becoming friends. It pains me to think of how many years we wasted—I wasted—not getting to know the people around us.

The world is filled with fascinating people. I wish you could see them as I do. At the same time, I wish I could bring myself to be the perfect daughter you always envisioned.

Had I the power to turn back time, I would return to when the day's hurts could be cured with an embrace and a kiss from you.

I love you, and I miss you.

Your loving daughter,

Marina

***

Dear Papa,

I love you and I miss you and Mama and Gabriel very deeply. My relationship with Jackson is complicated to say the least, but what transpired between us must remain my burden to bear. There are much bigger issues to consider presently, including your health. How do you feel?

No doubt you have heard of my situation, but do not worry for me. I have several competent and wonderful people looking out for me. They are Arkonai, but they understand me and the way I see the world better than most of our people.

The Supreme Huntmaster and the prison warden are not

bad men. In their own way, they seek what is best for their people. I cannot fault them for that. The High Council wants justice for a tragedy and great crime committed against the village of River's Edge. For my own reasons, I cannot help them obtain this justice, so they keep me. I am eager to return to my work, but otherwise, I am content to patiently await their decision.

There is a small chance the High Council will deem my death a necessary substitute for true justice. Daniel frowns mightily at me for mentioning that, but I must. I do not say this to hurt you, but I also cannot leave words unsaid. The strong support I have received from people of every kind warms my heart and moves me to tears, but it also speaks of very strong feelings surrounding the situation. In that context, my death could lead to further conflict. Such a thing would undo every good thing I have ever done in this life. Please, do not let that happen.

That you have not cast me aside before now greatly comforts me. I do not fear death, for I know I will simply leave this troubled world behind for a better one. I fear becoming a rallying cry for those whose hearts are blinded by hatred. Do not let that happen. I will not cease to be your child because of any ceremony, but if such a ceremony can save lives, do it.

Papa, the One did not make us Arkonai, Saroth, and Bereft, only human. We chose those distinctions. The Arkonai may be wrong about many things, but they are right to believe that the Bereft deserve our protection and service. It's time the Saroth emerged from behind the magical barriers of Caramore and started righting the problems facing everybody.

If the whispers are true, the Outcast has renewed his efforts to reclaim Aeris, and there will soon come a time when people cannot afford the luxury of our divisions. We must unite and embrace every kind of magic and those who have none.

I am forever your loving daughter,

Mari

***

Dear Gabriel,

I hope you are well and staying away from Jackson. For all his bluster and threats, I believe somewhere deep down there is genuine affection within him, especially for you. When his anger subsides, he will pursue peace with you. Be wary of him, but don't be afraid to love him. He's still our brother, no matter what he's done.

Were this only about the inheritance he seems obsessed with, I would beg father to cast me aside and raise him up, but it's not. Jackson has an innate need to manipulate, to conquer, to win. He always has. Do you remember excluding him from our games when he played too rough? The same principle is in play, but we have moved far beyond childhood games.

His decisions have ruined many lives, but in a way, so have mine. I cannot condemn him without bearing some of the blame.

I am sorry we could not sort our differences without hurting you as well. As I said before, if what he presented in that contract was his final demand, I would pay his asking price, but a soul like his is never satisfied. I see this now.

Do what you must to keep Tielle and her family safe, even if that puts us at cross-purposes. Yet before you make any big decisions, seek wisdom from the One. I cannot make your decisions for you, but as your big sister, I must warn you that every decision you make will be one you have to live with.

All my love,

Marina

***

Dear Jackson,

I cannot help but think that I have failed you in some profound way for you to harbor such hatred for me. After our last encounter, anger and despair brought me very close to a dark place. I have tried to forgive you on my own and failed at it. Only the Lady's grace and the One's will delivered a measure of peace to me.

But can there be peace between us?

You have always had high ambitions, but try to remember that people matter more than any amount of wealth or power. Others who do not know you as I do may not see the changes in you, but I do. Your actions tell me you have embraced at least some of the Outcast's teachings. They are lies. He will promise you much and deliver little at too high a price. Please, see that before it's too late and the darkness blinds you to the things that would truly make you happy.

If we are destined for conflict, can we at least agree to leave Gabriel out of it? He should not have to pick a side between us. As increasingly impossible as it is to meet your demands, make them to me directly. Threatening him will only make me want to hurt you, and believe it or not, I actually know how to do so. I don't like feeling that way.

You are my brother, so you will always have my love. Can we forget what was done and move forward?

Your sister,

Marina

Chapter 17:
Crisis

Warden's Office, Northgate Prison

"Lady Christa Arrington," announces the taller of her two guard escorts. He steps aside so she can move past him into the office.

Warden Arthur Clark rises from the large chair situated behind his expansive desk.

"Welcome, Lady Christa," he greets. "I've been looking forward to this meeting for a long time. Please, sit. Make yourself comfortable."

"I should get home soon," says Christa. "It's been a long day."

Her gaze fixes on the antlers springing out of the warden's chair. She'd always hated that chair. She has never quite understood the fascination some hunters have with taking trophies from their conquests.

The door clicks shut behind her.

"The men told me you hardly miss a visit," comments the warden. "That business with Guardsman Roland was unfortunate. How is our Saroth guest faring today?"

"She's eager to try writing again, but Master Cordova insists she rest the hand another week or two," answers Christa. She idly wishes they could just apply Healer Gifts, but Master Cordova insists that since the injury was caused by magic, the use of it could make matters worse. "The wounds are almost completely healed, but her range of motion is still poorer than it ought to be at this stage. I'm going home to see if I have any herbs that might help her."

"Stay a while. Your uncle is on his way," says Warden Clark. "I'm sure he'd love to see you."

One of the guards steps up beside Christa and takes hold of her left elbow.

Confusion and surprise prevent Christa from responding verbally, but she instinctively pulls her arm away from the man and steps to her right.

The other guard catches her and shoves her forward.

After two stumbling steps, Christa catches the back of a guest chair to steady herself. Straightening, she stares at the warden. Only her intense grip on the back of the chair indicates her sudden unease.

"Cooperation is in your best interest, and that of our Saroth guest," says the warden, smiling pleasantly.

"She's under Council pro—" Christa begins.

"Yes. Yes. Council protection," the warden finishes. He waves his right hand dismissively. "But you see, they will soon be busy with a little crisis I'm creating for them."

The guard who shoved Christa guides her around the chair and forces her to sit.

"That means I'll be free of their meddling oversight for a time," explains Warden Clark. "Prisons are very difficult to control sometimes. Mix-ups happen. Certain pampered prisoners can suddenly find themselves in the general population."

"They'll murder her." Christa whispers the horrifying conclusion. Rising panic causes her breaths to quicken.

"They'll do far worse to her first," promises the warden.

Christa breathes deeply, trying to get her mind working again.

"What kind of cooperation are you looking for?" asks Christa. She longs to infuse the question with defiance and anger, but her shaking body barely parts with them as a whisper.

"Your presence mostly," replies Warden Clark. "Should you survive the day, I would be delighted if you married my nephew, Garok."

The last statement sends Christa's thoughts racing. A certain amount of wealth and prestige awaits her future husband, but those benefits come with the heavy responsibilities of running the Shadow Oaks estate and associated businesses.

There is no political advantage unless something happens to her uncle.

She flinches and tries to stand, but one of the guards holds her in place by pressing down on her shoulders.

"You're going to kill him," Christa says.

"I'm going to *have* him killed." The warden calmly corrects her. "But those are details that only those of us in this room will be privy to.

Officially, our esteemed Supreme Huntmaster will fall afoul of Saroth assassins."

A loud pounding at the door prompts Christa to twist her head left as horror spreads throughout her whole body.

"He's early," comments Warden Clark. He waves impatiently to one of the guards.

The man races to open the door.

The other ceases holding Christa's shoulders down and instead pulls her out of the chair. In one motion, the guard turns Christa toward the door and shoves her so that she stumbles into the free space between the chairs and the entry.

Suddenly, a rope materializes around her and pulls tight, pinning Christa's arms to her sides. She cries out as her forward motion carries her to the ground. Landing with a grunt, Christa fights for her next few breaths as the conjured rope adjusts to her new position.

The shorter guard swings the door open, revealing the Supreme Huntmaster.

"Uncle Ash! Run!" Christa shouts.

A long sword appears in Ashton Casse's hands, causing the guard who answered the door to back up slowly.

"Ashton, we've been waiting for you," calls the warden. "Please, come in. Shut the door behind you. This transaction requires some privacy."

Christa watches her uncle absorb the scene quickly. His gaze lands on her only briefly before moving up to the warden.

"I'm here now," says Uncle Ash calmly. He's still holding the shorter guard at bay with his sword. "You may let Christa leave while we discuss these matters like men."

The guard uses the enchanted rope around Christa to pull her up to a standing position. He doesn't level a weapon at her, but it's clear the rope itself is a weapon in the Guardian's magical grip.

Christa silently pleads with her uncle to flee, but she knows it's futile. He would never abandon her.

"She is joining us today to ensure you follow directions very carefully," explains Warden Clark.

"And what would you like me to do?" Uncle Ash inquires.

Christa has heard huntsmen whisper of her uncle's bravery, but she has never seen him display such before this moment. Before her parents' deaths, he had been the mysterious uncle who disappeared for months at a time, only to reappear triumphantly with a small gift for her.

After an outbreak of Braiser's Disease killed them within a week of each other, he had petitioned the High Council for a leave so he could help her transition to the new reality.

She turns sideways so she can see the warden's face as he responds.

Warden Clark picks up an egg-shaped object off his desk and holds it up with both hands as if presenting an offering.

Christa vaguely recalls seeing it before.

"In a few moments, we're going to be ambushed by a pair of Saroth assassins," the warden says. "We're going to fight valiantly. I'll even suffer a few wounds, but you won't survive." He speaks to Uncle Ash while still admiring the object in his hands.

Christa turns her attention back to her uncle.

His expression doesn't change much, but he lets his gaze linger on her.

"And what of my niece?" he asks.

"She'll be perfectly safe with my men," says the warden. He nods to the guard controlling the enchanted rope.

Christa tries to resist, but the rope pulls her off to the left side of the room as one enters As her back slams into the wall, she remembers where she saw the strange object before. It came with several gifts for Marina. Dread fills her.

Whatever it holds will lead back to Marina!

The guards follow, taking up flanking positions beside her.

Warden Clark tosses the egg-like object over his desk. It lands with a solid thud. The entire top half folds open, and two brown beetles emerge. One beetle scurries left of the capsule, while the other speeds in the opposite direction.

Shapeshifters!

As the thought appears in Christa's mind, two figures dressed in form-fitting black outfits appear simultaneously. Both men are relatively small with short, jet-black hair. They carry no weapons, but there is a menacing quality to their serious expressions.

The guards with Christa each retrieve a dagger from the sheaths at their waist and toss it to one of the strangers.

"Kill him first," instructs Warden Clark. "Then we can stage the rest."

"It won't work," says Uncle Ash. He sounds almost bored. "Any first-year Seeker can read a room's history. Give me my niece, and we'll forget this … indiscretion."

The warden's feral smile sickens Christa.

"I'm touched by your concern, but my Council contact has that part well in hand," he says.

A choking noise sounds from either side of Christa. Whipping her head left, she spots one of her guards clutching his neck where a tiny throwing dagger pokes out between his fingers. He falls over dead. Shaken, she looks back to her uncle, not daring to look at the other guard. She hadn't even seen her uncle move. The ropes around her loosen and fall to the floor.

"Christa, go," says her uncle. He keeps the sword leveled between the two Saroth men.

"Come with me," she says.

"I'll be right behind you." Her uncle's voice is reassuring.

"No!" cries the warden. Reaching into his desk, he pulls out a small crossbow and points it at Christa.

A split-second later, the weapon spits two small bolts at her. She screams.

Two clang-thunk noises sound as the bolts hit the wall near her head, redirected there by more throwing daggers.

"Hurry up and kill him," Warden Clark snaps at the assassins. "He should almost be out of daggers by now."

The assassins spread out, trying to split her uncle's attention.

Fear closes Christa's throat and keeps her rooted in place.

"Sunny," calls Uncle Ash, using a nickname he hasn't uttered in years. "I'm going to have to ask you to leave now."

The nickname as much as the weariness in his tone, chills her, but she takes a step toward the door, then two.

Pain slashes through her upper left arm, and she suddenly feels lightheaded. The bolt that struck her continues on and smashes a painting next to the door.

"That bolt contains a contact poison," says Warden Clark. "Are you listening, Ashton? You have a choice to make, and I suggest you make it quickly. Christa gets the antidote as soon as you're dead. If you delay, she'll die in a matter of minutes."

Sparks of light dance on the edges of Christa's vision. There's a small tear in her sleeve but relatively little blood. Despite this, strength drains from her rapidly. Her knees buckle.

Something heavy hits the ground, and her uncle appears before her in time to catch her.

"I've got you, Sunny," says Uncle Ash. He eases her to the floor and leans over her. "You'll be fine."

Fighting through a dull headache, Christa looks up at her uncle. Two figures loom above him.

"Fight them," Christa mumbles.

"Can't," he answers. "You've got to live. I promised my baby sister I'd protect her little girl, and so I am."

Her tears flow freely.

He brushes them aside with his thumbs, but more take their place. Gently, he covers her eyes with his hands, pulling her eyelids down.

"You are stronger than you know, and I love you for it. But I want you to keep your eyes closed until this is over."

She doesn't have long to wait.

A sickening crack sounds.

His hands fall away from her face.

Christa's eyes fly open, but her head feels too heavy to move.

Her uncle's body lies beside her, but she dares not look at it. If these are to be her final moments, she wishes to face them bravely like Uncle Ash would want her to.

The two assassins stand above her.

"Thank you for your service," says Warden Clark. "Your reputation is well-deserved. The rest of the payment will be sent as agreed."

"Give her the antidote," says the assassin on Christa's right.

"Let her die," says the warden dismissively. "She's more trouble than she's worth."

"You made a verbal contract with the Supreme Huntmaster," explains the other assassin. "You must honor it."

"We're done. You can leave now." Warden Clark's tone hardens. "I have a lot of work to do."

Through blurry vision, Christa sees the assassins exchange a significant look.

Together, they make flinging motions.

A cry rings out from the warden.

A short time later, a small vial gets pressed to Christa's lips.

"Drink," instructs the first assassin. "This will destroy the poison." He gently holds her jaw open and pours in the liquid.

"Don't try to move for a few minutes," says the second assassin. "You'll be weak and disoriented, but it will fade in about half an hour."

"Why?" Christa asks weakly. She means the question quite a few different ways. Why did they kill her uncle? Why did they spare her? Why did they kill the warden?

"He broke a contract," explains the second assassin. "Your life for you uncle's."

The assassins stand then vanish from Christa's sight. The droning sound of insect wings beating the air fills her ears as she leans her head back to gather the strength to rise.

I must warn Daniel and Marina!

Chapter 18:
No Peace

Jackson's Office, Castaloni Estate, City of Dominance

No, there cannot be peace between us, Marina. You need to die so I can reach my full potential. I am tired of living in your shadow. Father still believes you can do no wrong. When your use to my Master ceases, I will kill you and everyone who tries to stop me.

Jackson Castaloni crumples his sister's letter and sets it on fire with his fingertips. He cradles it in his hands until the parchment is reduced to ashes.

"And I will use Gabriel as I like," he declares, brushing his hands against each other. Speaking of such, he figures it's time to check in with his brother. Odds are good the report will be much the same as the previous dozen, but Jackson needs to see someone following orders.

Touching the Keeper's pendant hanging from his neck, Jackson speaks the spell that will allow him to communicate with his brother.

"What do you want?" Gabriel's tone is decidedly hostile.

"What is the latest news?" Jackson inquires, keeping his voice pleasant.

"You know everything I do," says Gabriel. "Marina's still in prison, Marcus won't let me see her, and Tielle sides with him on that point. She thinks the Arkonai might try to imprison me if they find out who I am."

"But the merry little rescue band has met a few times in the past month, has it not?" Jackson knows they have since he monitors his brother's movements closely through a series of Minders and servants looking for some extra coin. "Your report on the last meeting was suspiciously like the one before. Surely, something of note transpired."

"Adaram says next to nothing, and Gabriella and Marcus have been distracted with wedding details," Gabriel explains. "The escape plan options have not changed much, and the main issue with any of them is Marina's cooperation, which we're not getting."

"She wishes to stay in the Arkonai prison?" Jackson's inflection makes it a question. The few visits he has made to Dawtan Prison in Temperance have convinced him no sane person would ever wish such a fate on themselves. He can't imagine Arkonai prisons being any nicer than ones in the neutral city.

"Of course not, but she refuses any plan that involves others." Gabriel says impatiently. "Which is all of them."

"That sounds like her," Jackson mutters. She likely can't stand the thought of needing help or endangering another person. "But do you need her consent in order to rescue her?"

A sharp intake of breath and several seconds of silence are Gabriel's answer.

"You never considered that," Jackson says, surprised such a thing would elude two such vaunted Minders as Gabriella Ricci and Marcus Polani.

"Jackson, you're brilliant!"

Gabriel's exclamation pleases Jackson. He hasn't heard such a hopeful tone from his brother in a very long time.

"But why do you want her free?" Suspicion and dread characterize Gabriel's question. "I thought you wanted her dead so you can inherit."

I do.

"Wishing she were not Father's heir does not mean I relish the thought of her in a filthy prison," Jackson replies, opting for a response that will not anger his little brother.

"Marcus says her cell is clean and comfortable," Gabriel assures him. "I had expressed similar concerns."

"That's good to hear," Jackson says automatically. Internally, he indulges in a private moment of frustration.

Why does everything always seem to go her way?

"Yes, it's a relief to know," Gabriel agrees, "but we must still free her or there will be more incidents like the one with the guard who tried to kill her."

"Tell me about that," Jackson orders. A different source already informed him of the attack a few weeks ago, but he needs to know what Gabriel will say and not say to gauge his level of cooperation.

"A guard tried to kill her, but a friend stepped in and fought him," Gabriel reports.

"Don't you find the timing convenient?" Jackson wonders. He steps around his desk and crosses to the far side of the room because moving helps him think. "Who was this friend with excellent timing?"

Gabriel hesitates.

Jackson sighs.

"I already know it was Daniel Saveron," he informs his brother darkly. "And you'll have to do a lot better telling your stories if you want to protect dear Tielle."

"Stop threatening her."

"Stop wasting my time," Jackson fires back. "This next question's an easy one but I expect complete honesty from you. I've been told Marina was wounded in that incident. What happened?"

Silence descends again, but Jackson patiently waits. Gabriel has always possessed a terrible reputation when it comes to holding back details of anything.

"After the guard attacked her, Daniel appeared and fought him, but the fight was not going well," Gabriel explains at last. "Marina broke the security enchantment so more guards would come. The thing nearly severed her wrist before they could deactivate it."

The notion of her pain doesn't please Jackson as much as he thought it would.

"Why would she do something like that?" Jackson wonders. He can guess, but he needs to hear Gabriel's thoughts on the matter.

"He's her friend," Gabriel answers.

"Are you sure that's all he is to her?" Jackson presses.

"Wait. You think she has feelings for the huntsman," Gabriel says. He sounds like the concept never occurred to him.

"Forget what I think. What do you think?" Another question pops into Jackson's head and out his mouth before he gets an answer from his brother. "Would she marry him and mix the magic lines? You know how dangerous that could be."

"Nobody knows what would happen," Gabriel argues weakly.

"You've heard the prophecies," says Jackson.

"I have," Gabriel admits. "They speak of great change, but that doesn't mean it's a bad thing."

"Gabriel, those prophecies could mean the end of the world," says Jackson. "Do you want to be responsible for that?"

"No, but how did this suddenly become about me?" Gabriel asks.

"Kill him."

Jackson lets the order stand through the predictable moment of silence.

"I doubt I could if I tried," says Gabriel.

"Get close to the huntsman. He trusts you. Learn to use that trust to your advantage," Jackson instructs. "When he lets down his guard, poison his water or—"

"Is that what you did to Father?" Gabriel interrupts.

"What?" Jackson can't help the question. He searches his mind for any slipup that would have revealed the truth to his brother. "Why would you say such a thing?"

"Marina thinks you poisoned him," says Gabriel.

"We've discussed this before," Jackson says, irritated. "Until Father casts Marina aside in favor of me as his heir, he's perfectly safe from me."

"I used to believe that."

Gritting his teeth, Jackson deliberately delays responding. The flippant, defiant notes in Gabriel's answer disturb him. They're a very bad sign. Soon, a moment will come when the boy will have to pick a side, and if he chooses wrong, Jackson will have no choice but to punish him.

"What can I say to make you believe me?" Jackson asks.

"Swear on Mother's life," says Gabriel.

"Fine," Jackson agrees. Sudden unease grips his stomach even as he voices the lie.

"Thank you." Genuine relief floods the two words. "What do you think is wrong with Father? Is it caused by poison or a disease? Could it be one of the rival houses or is the One calling him home?"

"I have not visited him for a few days," Jackson says. "You know more about his condition than I do."

"Last I saw him was two days ago," Gabriel reports. "He was barely conscious for much of the visit." He pauses for a long stretch before softening his tone. "If you wish to see him again, you should do so soon."

The statement alarms Jackson. The servant who keeps him informed from the Outreach estate had given him a favorable report only yesterday.

Somebody's lying to me, but who?

Absently, Jackson promises to visit their parents and ends the communication with his brother. He needs to think. His man inside the estate was supposed to stop delivering the poison some time ago, but did he do so?

Chapter 19:
Go

Marina's Cell, Northgate Prison, City of Aridel

"How do Shapeshifters discover their animal forms?" Daniel wonders. He lounges back in the wooden chair beside the bed, taking a break from his afternoon scribing duties. "Is there any choice involved?"

"I'm not sure," Marina answers. "Sometimes, it's by accident, and other times, it's only after intense study." She chuckles as a memory comes to her. "My brother, Gabriel, first became a squirrel when he was a muddy toddler trying to avoid a bath. That was an interesting chase. He spent much of it running back and forth across the ceiling, leaving tiny mud prints everywhere."

She misses those days.

Daniel's rich laughter joins hers.

"How did they catch him?" he asks.

"My parents and three servants covered every exit from the room with blankets or curtains. Then, they held out a blanket stretched between them and begged him to come down."

"Did it work?" Daniel wonders.

"Sort of," Marina reports. "I ... helped a bit by firing a weakened lightning bolt near him. It didn't hurt him, but he leapt far enough to miss the blanket and land on Olivia. She was not pleased, nor was my mother. I think that might be the only time I saw—"

Marina cuts herself off and stares at the figure suddenly standing before her cell's door. A heavy, hooded cloak prevents immediate recognition, but as the figure fumbles with the lock, the hood shifts and reveals long blond hair.

Daniel twists his head right to follow Marina's gaze.

"Christa!" Daniel scrambles to his feet and faces the door. "What's wrong?"

Only after Daniel voices the question, does Marina see the expression Christa Arrington wears. She looks like she's walked through a room full of Darkland creatures. Her left arm is tucked across her stomach. She has placed the key into the lock, but her trembling right hand struggles to turn it.

"You have to leave!" Christa declares. "Both of you. Right now."

Finally, the lock clicks open, and Christa rushes in.

By this time, Marina has risen from the bed.

Daniel catches Christa's shoulders and braces her. He moves to pull her into a comforting embrace, but she smacks him in the chest.

"Don't!" she cries. "If you comfort me now, I will fall to pieces and fail to explain what I need to."

The thick tear tracks and streaks of red running up and down her face tell them she's crumbling rapidly.

"What happened?" asks Marina.

Christa squeezes her eyes shut and lets her shoulders sag.

"They killed him."

Daniel quickly guides her to the bed and lowers her to a sitting position.

"Killed who?" he prompts, kneeling before his friend.

Sitting beside Christa, Marina pulls her into a hug.

"Just cry," she says. "We're here for you."

Christa sucks in sharply when Marina touches her left arm.

Casting an alarmed look at Daniel, Marina flips the cloak's fabric away from Christa's arm. She finds the sleeve of the light blue dress torn. The wound doesn't appear to be very deep, but there's an unhealthy, green tinge to the skin around it. Dried blood runs down the sleeve to Christa's wrist.

Gingerly, Marina touches Christa's arm immediately above the wound. Heat radiates through the sleeve. Moving her good hand up to Christa's forehead, Marina confirms the fever.

"Grab her legs," she orders Daniel.

Turning Christa, Marina guides her to a prone position on the bed.

"Please! I have to tell you! Leave. Soon." Christa's voice grows weaker but increasingly desperate with each phrase.

"First, we deal with this problem," says Daniel. He draws a

dagger from the Veil along with a few clean rags and some bandages. Quickly, he folds one of the rags into a thick band. "Put this in her mouth, hold her steady, and don't look." Daniel hands Marina the rag he had folded.

Following the instructions, Marina tucks the rag into place and leans across Christa's shoulders.

Her friend's eyes plead with her to reconsider.

"He has to clean the wound," Marina explains. "I'm sorry."

Space gets tight because Daniel needs to climb up onto the bed and move past Marina to access Christa's left arm.

Despite the warning not to look, Marina watches Daniel slash across the wound several times, widening it from above, below, and along both sides. Christa screams into the gag and fresh tears spill out.

"He's almost done," Marina encourages, hoping she speaks truth.

"I am done," says Daniel. "I removed what I could. The bleeding should do the rest of the cleansing. I'll wrap it shortly."

Oddly, the physical pain has calmed Christa. There's a new clarity in her gray-green eyes. She shakes her head and tries to say something through the rag.

"Can I remove the gag now?" Marina asks, directing the question to Daniel.

He nods.

Marina does so and then grips Christa's free hand with her good one.

"We're listening," she promises.

Christa draws several deep, shaky breaths before launching into her tale.

"The warden used me to trap my uncle and kill him."

"Why would he do that?" Marina wonders. She looks from Christa to Daniel, trying to predict who will explain first.

Daniel's expression clouds with worry and suppressed rage, but he says nothing as he quickly wraps Christa's arm.

She merely shakes her head.

"Too many reasons to list," says Christa. "It doesn't matter. He's dead now, and you must leave soon." She locks eyes with Marina.

"Why is he dead?" Marina knows Warden Arthur Clark hadn't been her staunchest supporter, but she can't understand why his death has anything to do with her. "And what does that have to do with me?"

"My uncle's assassination involved two Saroth Shapeshifters,"

Christa explains.

"But you said the warden hired them," Daniel argues. "Any Seeker could get the truth from the room's history."

"Uncle Ash made that argument," says Christa, not bothering to shift her attention to Daniel. "The warden laughed and indicated that somebody from within the High Council would handle the cover-up."

"Who would do that?" Daniel's tone indicates his disbelief. Having finished his work on Christa's arm, he shuffles backward off the bed and stands up.

"I will find that out," Christa vows, "but the pressing concern is getting the two of you away." She squeezes Marina's left hand tightly. "The assassins came in one of the gifts delivered for you. I thought nothing of it at first because the warden kept quite a few things back, but now that he is dead, the situation could not be worse for you."

"Blame for both of their deaths will fall to the Saroth," Daniel concludes. "That means you. She's right. We must get you away from Aridel."

"I—"

"Please, Marina," Christa says, cutting off the protest. She pours much of her remaining strength into her next words. "Go. You are one of the only friends I have had in a long time. I will clear your name. I promise, but we won't get that chance if you're still in this prison when the Council hears of these deaths."

"There will be crowds demanding retribution even before the facts are known," Daniel explains. "The High Council may choose to appease them by handing you over." He doesn't need to elaborate any further.

"Would it work?" Marina asks softly. She's not eager to die, but she would rather one life be sacrificed if others would be spared.

"No." Daniel's answer is short and emphatic.

"Your death would only be the first of many." Christa's declaration destroys the last of Marina's resistance to the idea of escape.

"What's your plan?" Marina asks Christa.

"Same as we discussed before," she answers. "Except instead of Gabriella staying in your place, it will be me." Reading the dismay that washes over Marina, Christa hurries on. "My uncle's death will garner a lot of sympathy for me in the Council. I am perhaps the only person who can do this for you."

Pulling her hand free, Christa reaches into an inner pocket of the cloak and withdraws a small, thin object and holds it out for Daniel.

Marina recognizes it as the device that will deactivate the enchanted security bracelet.

"I stole this from Master Cordova," Christa says, as she slowly sits up. "Hurry and get it transferred."

Daniel directs Marina to sit in the chair. When she does so, he waves the device over each of the crystals in the bracelet. They darken one by one. When the last one blinks out, there's a faint clicking noise and the bracelet falls free. Catching it, Daniel quickly loops it around Christa's right wrist and reactivates the enchantment. The bracelet conforms to Christa's wrist.

Cradling the newly liberated wrist with her other hand, Marina relishes the empty, weightless feeling. Something invisible lifts off her soul.

Being careful not to hit Christa's left arm, Marina pulls her up into a tight embrace.

"Thank you for everything. I'm sorry for your loss, and I'm sorry you have to be strong right now," says Marina.

"Thank me by living," Christa replies. She returns the hug one-armed before gently pulling away.

Marina steps back so Daniel can take her place and hug Christa. Their embrace is short, but Christa's good hand lingers on his shoulder. Marina can't see his face from this angle, but there's a new kind of sadness in Christa's expression.

"Take care of her, Daniel." The charge comes out soft but firm. She lets her hand fall away from his shoulder.

"I will get her somewhere safe and return to explain things to the Council," Daniel says.

"Leave them to me," Christa insists. "They will heed me eventually, but in the meantime, they will hunt for you. Be vigilant and get out of the city soon. Go somewhere else as far and as fast as you can."

"As you wish, but at least, let me send Jordan to help," Daniel pleads.

Christa agrees to the idea.

"It's best I don't know where you go, but I can direct you out of the prison," Christa says. "When you leave the cell, go right and make your way to the portal room. If anybody challenges you, tell them you've been summoned to the Council. Step through the portal to Bastion and then choose a different portal. Holt is guarding the door to the warden's office, but he cannot delay the discovery forever. Get going."

They take a step toward the cell's door.

"Wait. Take the cloak," Christa says, reaching for the clasp. "They must not see your hand free of the bracelet."

Daniel helps Christa climb out from under the cloak and throws it around Marina's shoulders. The heavy fabric feels like it carries extra warmth and protection from Christa.

Thank you, my friend. May the One and the Lady give you strength through your grief.

Chapter 20:
By Your Side

Master Gibbs's Office, Castaloni Shipping Headquarters, Kaltan City

"Marina, please eat something," says Daniel. "It's been hours since the midday meal, and depending on how this goes, we could have a long way to travel tonight."

"What is taking so long?" Marina wonders, ignoring Daniel's plea. Her restless steps carry her back and forth across the empty space in front of the long conference table.

One end of the table bears several trays of cold meats, breads, and cheeses. Master Gibbs, the manager of this facility, had been about to begin his evening meal when they arrived. Once he grasped their situation, he'd sent his assistant to fetch more food. They had used the waiting time to explain their desire to contact Marina's brother, Gabriel.

"It has only been about three minutes," Daniel notes. Idly, he picks up a small roll. Truthfully, he doesn't feel like eating either, given the events of the day, but he understands the danger of not eating when they can. "Judging from the size of this place and guessing he'll carry the message personally, he's probably just arrived at his destination."

Marina shoots him an exasperated look.

"I know," she admits, "but every second we delay increases the possibility of discovery. I don't want to place these people in danger any longer than necessary." Frustrated, she stops pacing and bows her head. "I shouldn't have come here, but I need to speak with Gabriel. I must know what happened to my father."

"I've been thinking about that, and I believe I have a plan," says

Daniel. Tossing the small roll up into the air, he waits for it to fall and catches it deftly. "I will share my thoughts if you sit down and eat." He waves the roll slowly from side to side before deliberately taking a large bite out of it.

A steady stare from Marina tells him she's measuring his sincerity. Sighing deeply, she trudges over to the table and stiffly sits in the chair to Daniel's left. He occupies the end position closest to the door.

Plucking up a wheat roll, Marina tears off a small chunk and eats it.

Daniel nudges a glass of water closer to her.

"It's a tad dry," he comments.

"You promised me a plan," Marina says, picking up the water glass and taking a sip.

"You're certain your father was poisoned, but you have no proof," Daniel begins, stating the conclusions they had drawn together from the scant details provided by Gabriella and Marcus on their visits. "I don't know if I can get you tangible proof others would believe, but there is a way for you to know the truth. The main question is: do you want to know?"

"Of course, I do." The uncertainty in Marina's eyes contradicts the conviction in her voice. She nibbles on a few more bread morsels. "At least, I think I do. What did you have in mind?"

"I'm a Seeker," Daniel says. "My Gifts allow me to read a room's history. It's not always perfect, but I should be able to glimpse enough to let you know for certain."

Desperate hope flashes into her eyes.

"If I knew the poison, I might be able to reverse it!" Marina exclaims. The hope fades. "But that would require you being present in the room with my father."

"Don't you think he'll like me?" Daniel smiles briefly to let her know it's not a serious question.

"I think he'd love you." Marina's soft response surprises him. "But if he's as ill as Marcus reports, there will be guards on his room."

"Could your brother get us Teleportation scrolls that carry us into his room?" Daniel asks.

"Maybe, but you're missing the point," says Marina. "It will be dangerous."

"All of life is dangerous," Daniel reminds her. "That doesn't mean we stop living."

Growing quiet, Marina tears the rest of the roll to pieces and spreads the fragments around her plate. Twice, she opens her mouth to speak, only to frown and say nothing.

"Daniel, I'm grateful for your friendship and aid these past few months, but—"

"I'm not leaving you," Daniel says, cutting her off. He reaches out and stills her hands with a touch. He forces another smile. "I did once and look what a mess that was."

Laughing shortly, Marina raises her eyes to meet his. Hers shine bright with unshed tears.

"Don't you want a peaceful life?" she asks, turning her palms up to hold his hands.

The touch of her damaged hand is noticeably cooler than its counterpart.

"I want a life with you." Daniel feels the truth of those words spread throughout his whole body. Standing and releasing her hands, he steps around the table.

She turns sideways in the chair as he kneels before her.

"I love you, Marina Castaloni," Daniel declares, picking up her hands again. "I don't know when that happened, and I don't care. I want your problems to be my problems, and I want to spend the rest of my life by your side. Will you marry me?"

"Others will hate the idea," Marina points out.

Rising, Daniel uses their clasped hands to pull Marina up and tucks his arms around her.

"This isn't about others," says Daniel. "It's about us, and the only answer I care about is yours." Uncertainty strikes him. "I ... know I don't have much to offer you, but—"

Marina ends his speech by pulling his head down until their lips meet. The kiss starts out soft and sweet but deepens as it continues.

Daniel didn't have much of a planned speech anyway, but soon, words in general elude him.

Finally, the need to breathe causes them to end the kiss.

Terrified, she means the kiss as a farewell, Daniel keeps his arms locked around Marina and rests his forehead on hers.

"Was that your answer?" he whispers. "I liked it, but can you put it into words, too?"

Chuckling, Marina kisses him softly again.

"Yes, that was my answer, and yes, I will marry you, Daniel Saveron." Turning her head sideways, Marina rests her head on his chest.

"I doubt I could get rid of you if I tried."

The enormity of what transpired settles on Daniel, causing him to tighten his hold on Marina.

"What's wrong?" Marina asks, pulling back far enough to look at his face.

"Nothing," he mumbles, "but there are a lot of details we need to sort."

"Agreed, but you did solve one of our problems," says Marina. Breaking his hold, she sits down and motions for Daniel to do the same. Gathering up most of the bread fragments, Marina eats them quickly before explaining. "We now have a reason to see my father together."

The idea sends a chill through Daniel.

Reaching out, Marina places a comforting hand on Daniel's arm.

"I will seek his blessing for our union as tradition demands," she says quietly.

"And if he denies you?" Daniel works hard to keep his voice steady.

"He won't," Marina promises. "If there's anybody in my family who understands my heart, it's my father."

"But what if he does?" Daniel insists. He doesn't wish to turn this into an argument, but he must have an answer.

"I promise you he won't," Marina repeats. "But to answer the hypothetical what if, I am very good at choosing my own path, regardless of what good sense or tradition may say."

"Am I not the path good sense leads you to?" Daniel teases.

"You are the path my heart chooses," Marina answers. She pats his arm before reaching for a piece of cheese. She eats it before speaking again. "We both know it's chosen trouble before."

Their conversation takes a lighter turn throughout the rest of the meal.

By the time they finish, Master Gibbs returns with a Minder who can relay a message to Gabriel Castaloni. While Marina dictates the message for the Minder, Daniel observes Master Gibbs. Sweat beads up on the man's forehead. From the moment they had met, nervousness radiated from the manager, but he seems worse now.

Drawing on his Gifts, Daniel quiets his soul and reaches into the room's past. In his mind's eye, he witnesses dozens of people come and go from the office over the past few months. It doesn't take him long to find a familiar face.

The shock of recognition carries Daniel to his feet.

"Marina, we need to go." Daniel doesn't bother masking his urgency.

"I'm sorry," says Master Gibbs hoarsely, drawing a dagger. "He said to keep you here until he arrived."

"Who?" Marina questions, leaning back in her chair. Her expression carries weariness and sadness, but not surprise. She had been sitting at the table conferring with the Minder.

The young girl wisely ducks under the table.

"Jackson," Daniel supplies.

"He will soon be master of the whole estate. I must obey him," says Master Gibbs. "Please, forgive me."

"There's nothing to forgive," Marina assures the man, rising from the chair. "But what do you know of my father's health?"

"Only that he is not long for the world, my lady."

When Master Gibbs lowers his head while addressing Marina, Daniel leaps forward and snatches the dagger away from the man. In another second, he has the dagger pointed back at the man's heart.

"Don't hurt him!" Marina cries.

A whimper comes from the child under the table.

Kneeling, Marina calls to the girl.

"It's all right, Penny," she says soothingly. "When we're gone, come on out and comfort your father. He needs you." She gazes up at Master Gibbs as she says these last words.

"I'll leave the dagger with the guard at whichever exit we take," Daniel says to Gibbs. He pulls the weapon back so it's no longer threatening the manager.

Still keeping his attention on the man, Daniel slides over to help Marina up.

"Tell my brother you tried your best, but we overwhelmed you," Marina instructs.

"He won't believe me," the manager says. His shoulders dip in defeat.

"Then, truly help me reach my father, and Jackson will never inherit." Strength flows through Marina's words.

"I'll help," says Penny from beneath the table. She crawls out and takes Marina's hand. "I'll carry your message." She looks expectantly at her father.

Gibbs nods permission.

Daniel thought she already had sent the message on, but Marina's relieved look tells him she wasn't fooled by the child's performance.

Closing her eyes to concentrate, the girl goes quiet for half a minute.

"It's done," she reports. "The Minder with Master Gabriel says he will meet you as arranged."

"We should leave then," says Marina.

"I'm sorry I didn't send the message right away. My father forbade it." The girl speaks the apology to Marina's feet.

Marina pulls the girl into a hug before replying.

"He wants to protect you, Penny. As long as you can, heed his words."

"Even if I know they're wrong?" Penny inquires. She takes a small step backwards.

"That's a heavy question," Marina comments. "You'll have to answer it for yourself someday. You're a Minder. You will know when the time is right. Sometimes, we have to fight for our fathers."

Daniel's not sure how he feels about the idea of meeting Marina's father, but if they want the truth behind the man's disease, they have to go to him.

I wonder if Gabriella and Marcus can help.

"Penny, can you reach Master Marcus Polani?" Daniel asks.

"I don't think so," the girl answers. "I'm not very good calling to new contacts."

"Please try," Marina encourages. She shoots Daniel a questioning glance. "If you clear your mind and think of his name several times, he may reach out to you. He too carries the Minder Gifts within him."

"What should I tell him?" wonders Penny.

"Tell him to meet us at the same time and location you sent Master Gabriel," Daniel instructs.

The task takes the girl much longer than contacting Gabriel, but she manages it.

Excitement crawls through Daniel's stomach like a living creature.

One way or another, they will have answers very soon.

Chapter 21:
Justice Done

High Council's Grand Meeting Chamber, Deliverance Hall, City of Bastion

This is foolishness.

I must be here. I need to see this.

Jackson Castaloni silently wages an argument with the Dark Man. The Master's thoughts appear like his own since there's no physical form for him to take on this mission.

If you're so concerned, warn me before the enchantment fails.

I am not your nursemaid, nor your servant.

Indeed not, Master, but I can better serve you amongst the living.

Getting no response, Jackson assumes he has temporarily won the disagreement. Somebody bumps into him from behind and mutters an apology. Before Jackson can respond, he gets jostled again from a different side. Pushing past the two men to his right, he seeks refuge in a semi-quiet corner. Fewer people vie for position here because it lacks a good view of the High Council members. That suits Jackson fine. He did not sneak into the Arkonai stronghold to view their stuffy leaders.

He came to see an execution.

Excitement zips through him as the wide double doors at the back slowly open and an announcer's voice rings out.

"Distinguished members of the High Council, Honorable Lords and Ladies, I present to you Lady Christa Arrington of Shadow Oaks and beloved niece of our late Supreme Huntmaster."

Every head drops as the Arkonai collectively mourn the Supreme Huntmaster's death. Lady Arrington's even, measured steps sound loud in the sudden silence.

Jackson's breath catches. Along his travels, he has seen many Arkonai and Bereft women, but this is his first time seeing the elite among them. His chosen vantage point gives him an excellent view of the beautiful woman.

Most of her blond hair has been swept up away from her neck, but several wavy strands flow down the sides of her face, forming an attractive frame. The color ranges from a crisp golden hue to a shade shy of pure white as dictated by the way the light streaming down from the skylights catches her hair. Her green eyes pass over the High Council members, pausing only an instant on the empty central chair. Her jaw trembles slightly even as her expression intensifies.

A pang of regret stabs Jackson, for he knows his actions have led to this young woman's pain.

Even enemies have family. Harden your heart against such weakness.

Thankfully, Lady Arrington speaks, saving Jackson the need to respond to his master.

"Thank you for coming," she begins, turning to address the large crowd pressed into both sides of the Grand Meeting Chamber. "I'm sure you have heard the reports from the Northgate Prison in the city of Aridel. It is true. My uncle is dead."

Many people speak at once, offering condolences and shouts of outrage.

Eventually, the lady's raised hands indicate her desire to continue.

"Friends, your support is much appreciated, but I have much to tell," says the lady. "Please, be patient while I explain what transpired."

"Who is responsible?" shouts one of the council members.

Jackson leans forward and spots the speaker since the small man's seat is located almost directly across from him.

Lady Arrington stares at the man for a full second.

"You are, Lord Wix."

Her announcement sets off another explosion of opinions both from the crowd and from the council members.

Is it true?

Jackson had known only that a powerful Arkonai worked to smooth the way for the assassins to get inside the Northgate Prison. He never had a name to refer to before.

Yes. Pay attention. If you can help him escape, do so, but

124

do not endanger yourself for it. He is dull but influential.

Every eye focuses on Lord Wix.

He laughs nervously.

"The girl is obviously distraught. It was a mistake to summon her for testimony so soon after Ashton's death."

"That's a very serious accusation, Lady Christa. Do you have any proof?" The question comes from a tall man with dark brown hair and light brown skin standing next to the accused man. He turns his body to face Lord Wix but makes no further move to threaten the man.

"I do, Master Ibish," replies Lady Christa. "I have several letters between Warden Arthur Clark and Lord Oleg Wix. These letters discuss the plan in great detail."

Lord Wix's features twist with scorn and triumph.

"Letters can be forged. They mean nothing."

"Letters can be forged," Lady Christa agrees, "but contracts cannot."

Lord Wix pales. Before anyone can move, the man draws a dagger from the folds of his robes and hurls it at the lady.

A flash momentarily blinds Jackson.

He doesn't see Master Ibish move, but next moment, the big man slides in front of Lady Christa and catches the dagger that would have pierced her neck had it landed.

"I think our path is clear," says Master Ibish calmly.

Two huntsmen step away from their wall posts and quickly bind Lord Wix's hands with thick metal shackles. They lead him down to the center area and shove him to his knees before Lady Christa and Master Ibish. The Huntmaster moves to the lady's side. The guards step back but remain close enough to intervene should the lady require further aid.

"Do you want to tell your story, or should we hear Lady Christa's testimony first?" asks Master Ibish.

Since the viewing platforms rise above the main floor, Jackson clearly sees Lord Wix's face go through several expressions. He starts out with fear, moves to contempt, switches to defiance, and finally settles back on contempt.

"I did what none of you had the guts to do," says Lord Wix. "I removed a weakness from our midst."

"That confirms your guilt, but it does not explain what you did. Do you care to unburden your soul before meeting your fate?" Huntmaster Ibish's voice isn't loud but there's gravity behind his question.

"He conspired with Warden Clark to hire Saroth assassins to kill my uncle and lay blame on an innocent woman," Lady Christa explains.

"She's not innocent," counters Lord Wix. "Despite what those lazy Seekers said. The Saroth girl deserves to die for walking these lands."

"That's not for you to say," notes Master Ibish.

"What did the Seekers say about Marina?" Lady Christa demands. A new fire enters her eyes. She turns to Huntmaster Ibish.

The big man lowers his head but holds his ground.

"She was cleared of the charges of wrongdoing in the village of River's Edge," he reports.

Lady Christa's cheeks burn red.

"When did this happen?"

"A few months ago." Lord Wix keeps his tone filled with mocking innocence. "The wheels of justice can be slow sometimes."

"Why was she still in prison?" Lady Christa pierces Master Ibish with a sharp look.

"I will explain the Council's decisions on that matter later, my lady," says Master Ibish. "But right now, we need to know the circumstances that deprived us of our leader and put ourselves on a course to raising our number back to five who will serve here in Bastion."

Jackson and the rest of the onlookers watch as Lady Christa gives a short but detailed account of events in Warden Clark's office.

"So, the real killers walk free," comments another of the High Council members. "Tell me, Lady Christa. Why would the Saroth assassins spare you?"

That man is Huntmaster Eric Dillworth. He might be a worthy successor for Wix. I will let you know.

"After wounding me with a poisoned crossbow bolt, Warden Clark presented the antidote as the prize for my uncle's life," says Lady Christa. "He paid that price, but the warden wanted to withhold the antidote anyway. To the assassins, that constituted a breach of contract. That is why he is dead, and how I came by the contract that hired them in the first place."

"I am satisfied. What say the rest of you?" Master Ibish looks to the other two members.

They echo his satisfaction. A nod to the two guards brings them forward. They yank Wix to his feet.

"Lord Oleg Wix, you stand accused and condemned of conspiring to murder Supreme Huntmaster Ashton Cassel, how do you plead?" asks Master Ibish. "Keep in mind, you have the right to seek a general court trial for your crimes, or you can plead with the man's next of kin for mercy. I suggest you take the latter path."

"I will," says Lord Wix reluctantly. "I am guilty."

"Speak directly to the lady and make your request," Master Ibish instructs.

Wix looks like he would rather eat a worm freshly dug from the ground.

"I do not regret saving our people from a weak Supreme Huntmaster, but I have no wish to die in torment either. Therefore, I humbly beg mercy from you."

"Mercy can take one of two forms, my lady," explains Master Ibish. "True mercy would be to let him choose his own end. False mercy would be to spare his life only to cast him in prison among those he helped condemn. Which will you grant him?"

"True mercy," answers Lady Christa.

"Then, I choose my death," Wix says with malice. "I wish to die by your hand, Lady Christa."

The crowd draws a collective breath and holds it.

Jackson doesn't quite understand the dynamics of what transpired, so his master explains.

If the lady does not kill him, he will go free.

Is she capable of such a thing?

We shall see.

Master Ibish slowly hands Lady Christa a dagger.

"The guards will hold him. You can strike him from the front or move behind him. I suggest slitting his neck from behind. It will be a much cleaner kill."

Lady Christa staggers and drops to her knees. The long, flowing gown she wears pools around her, creating a sea of purple-pink fabric around her. She lets the dagger slip from her grasp.

"I will not kill a man," she declares.

Lord Wix laughs.

"My lady, if you cannot fulfill his request, he will escape punishment for his crimes," explains Master Ibish.

"That's exactly the sort of weakness I fought," says Wix.

Tears cascade down Lady Christa's face, but she nods that she understands the consequences.

"So be it," whispers the lady.

"Let her call a champion," yells a man from the crowd.

Julie C. Gilbert

The noise level jumps as dozens of men beg to be allowed to take the lady's place as executioner.

A thoughtful look comes over Master Ibish. He raises both hands and calls for the crowd's attention.

"There may be a way!"

His announcement quiets the masses.

"The law is clear" cries Lord Wix. "She must kill me or free me."

Kneeling beside Lady Christa, Master Ibish gently picks up her hands.

"I believe we can see justice done and take a step to righting our numbers, but everything hinges on your next few words, my lady."

"She has no husband!" snaps Wix. "Nobody can champion her!"

"Not technically true," argues Huntmaster Eric Dillworth. "If she pledges herself to a man right now, he will become her intended and gain the right to champion any cause on her behalf."

"He would also be set to become the next Supreme Huntmaster," cries Wix. "Will you stand for that?"

"Aye, we would," replies Master Ibish, helping the lady to her feet. "Quickly, my lady, you must make a choice. If you have someone in mind, speak now. Otherwise, we will adjourn and have the eligible candidates present themselves to you on the morrow."

Everybody waits with anticipation.

Lady Christa looks dazed, but she dutifully scans the crowd. When she speaks, her voice comes out strong and clear.

"I pledge myself to Jordan Lekros."

Cheers and shouts of dismay cause Jackson's head to pound.

A young man is hustled forward and cast onto the main floor level from the viewer's platform on the opposite side. He lands on his feet.

"Do you accept this honor?" asks Master Ibish. "And do you understand what you must do to claim it?"

"I do on both accounts," answers the young man. With great ceremony, he drops to both knees before Lady Christa. "Christa Arrington, you have been my friend since childhood. It would be my greatest honor and privilege to be called your husband. May your troubles be mine forever. Will you consent to become my wife?"

"Yes." With that promise, Lady Christa seals the fate of her uncle's murderer.

128

Chapter 22:
Blessings

Antonio's Private Chambers, Castaloni Estate, City of Outreach
The Teleportation scroll provided by Gabriel does its job and delivers Marina directly into her father's bedchamber at the family's estate in Outreach. It's a large, well-appointed room lit softly by multiple energy orbs encased in glass jars mounted on the walls and hanging from the ceiling.

The two bodyguards standing at the foot of the large bed react swiftly by leaping forward and leveling thin swords at her.

Expecting this, thanks to Gabriel's warning, Marina stays on her knees and raises both hands in a non-threatening manner.

A third man rises from a chair next to the bed.

"Who dares disturb a dying man?" he demands.

The word *dying* pierces Marina.

"His daughter," she answers softly.

"Marina!" Surprise and delight fill the name. Her father's voice is weak but recognizable.

Hope, fear, and pain collide within her.

"Yes, Papa. I'm sorry I stayed away so long. May I see you in private?" Marina looks toward the bed even though she cannot see her father from the floor.

"Of course!"

"Antonio, we really need to finish this." says the man standing next to Papa's bed.

"Yes, yes, Mika. In good time," responds her father. "But I have not seen my daughter for years. Help me sit up. Then, take the guards and go. You may stand outside the door if you wish, but give me a few minutes alone with her. Is the scroll prepared to record my final wishes?"

"It is," Mika answers. "It's right here on the table. You should still have a witness or two, but it's enchanted to be legally binding once sealed with a drop of blood."

"Thank you, my friend," says Papa.

Marina's legs burn from kneeling so long, but she stays still while Mika Forester, her father's long-time legal counselor leaves with the guards.

As the door clicks shut behind them, Marina hurries to her father's side and reaches for his right hand. As soon as their hands clasp, her father pulls her into an embrace. The contact breaks down her emotional barriers, releasing tears. For a time, Marina simply rests in her father's arms, letting the gentle rise and fall of his chest comfort her.

Finally, she pulls away and sits on the edge of the bed, once again holding her father's right hand. The touch gives her a familiar, uneasy sensation. There's definitely poison at work in him.

If I had my Destroyer Gifts, I could save him.

The thought haunts her.

"I'm sorry, Papa." Her head dips with the weight of the words. "I cannot be the heir you deserve or desire." Several tears escape her efforts to curb them. "I can't even save you."

"You would fight the will of the One?" questions her father with a hint of amusement. "For it is He who commands the number of my days."

"No natural thing ails you," says Marina. "You were poisoned. I don't have proof yet, but if you let my friends join me, we can show you what happened."

"I know enough. ' Her father looks at her with deep sorrow and compassion. He places his left hand atop hers. "Having proof will change little."

"I would still like to try," says Marina. "There's someone I need you to meet anyway."

Her father gives her a long, measuring look.

"You may seek the truth on one condition. You must swear by the One and the Lady to tell no one of these matters."

"I do, and I will. But doesn't the guilty party deserve punishment?"

"If it turns out that one of your brothers arranged this poison, it would be an Unforgivable Crime," explains her father. He releases her hands and reaches for the scroll sitting on the table next to him.

Seeing what he wants, Marina gets up, retrieves the scroll, and presses it into his hands.

"What does that mean?" Marina wonders. She remains standing.

"It means that the Tariku League could extend punishment to your other brother, your mother, and you to discourage future attacks on the heads of noble houses." Her father pauses and meets her eyes. "Have you not wondered why such things are unheard of?" Smiling, he answers his own question. "Of course not. These are not things that should occupy a young woman's thoughts, especially one wishing to unite the whole of Aeris."

"You've read my letters?" Marina asks, somewhat startled that they even reached him. She sinks down onto the chair set beside the bed.

"Every word, many times," he assures her. Leaning further into the pillows propping him up, Papa sets the scroll in his lap and sighs. "My time is short, Mari. I only regret not seeing this vision of Aeris come to pass, but I believe in you. Now, what is your petition? Your beautiful eyes tell me you have one."

"Papa, I seek your blessing. I can endure many things, but not your disapproval in this matter." Marina leans forward eagerly. "I have come to love a man very deeply, and we wish to spend our lives together. I'd like you to meet him and let him seek the truth behind your condition. That is part of his Gift. Two others will help us see what he discovers."

"Ah. He must be an Arkonai Seeker then." Her father scrutinizes her expression. "Do you understand what you're getting into, love? Arkonai women do not have the same rights and opportunities granted to Saroth women." He raises a hand to forestall an argument. "Our society has many problems as well, but that is not the point. Is this man kind? Is he brave?"

"He has stood by me through much already," Marina replies.

"That is a start," says her father. "You will both face a lot of opposition. Are you prepared for that?"

"I don't know if I can answer that question," Marina says honestly.

"Summon him alone, please," instructs her father. "There are things I must say to you both before inviting others."

Closing her eyes, Marina folds her right hand over her heart and concentrates on calling to Daniel.

A moment later, he appears in the room a step behind her, having used one of his Seeker Gifts to answer her summons. It's not a popular aspect of the Seeker arts because it doesn't work over great distances and it takes a tremendous amount of energy to accomplish. Few wish to weaken themselves before an expected conflict.

Marina waves Daniel over.

He kneels next to her, keeping his head bowed as she had instructed him.

"Papa, this is Huntsman Seeker Daniel Saveron. In all my travels, I have not found a man with more honor than him." Marina stretches out her right hand for Daniel to take.

He does so, wrapping his hand around her wrist so she can feel the touch.

"Moreover, I love him very deeply," Marina adds. Shifting her eyes over to Daniel, she continues. "Daniel, this is my father, Antonio Castaloni."

"Do you feel the same as my daughter, huntsman?" asks her father.

"I do," Daniel answers without hesitation. His gaze rests on Marina. "She is unlike any other."

"Will you protect her?" asks Papa.

"With my life," Daniel confirms.

"Do you both understand the depths of anger and hatred such a union will stir?" inquires Papa. He moves his gaze evenly between them, finally settling on Marina. "Are you prepared for the consequences, whatever they may be?" His eyes plead with her to reconsider for her own sake.

"I don't know if anybody can truly be prepared for blind hatred," answers Marina, "but we will do our best."

"We will find a way," says Daniel.

"Then, help me face you," instructs Papa, setting aside the scroll.

With much effort, Marina and Daniel maneuver her father to a position where his legs can dangle over the side of the bed.

He bids them both to kneel, and they do. Then, he places his right hand on Marina's head and his left on Daniel's head before speaking.

"You have not chosen an easy path, dear children, but may the One and the Lady look favorably upon you. May you be blessed with many children to teach and train in ways that are right. May your love sustain you through opposition, and may there come a day when peace exists between the Arkorai and the Saroth. May your love begin to heal the old, divisive wounds."

A sense of warmth travels down from the top of Marina's head and spreads throughout her body. She senses the One's approval of her father's words.

Once he removes his hands from their heads, they help her father back to the position he started in propped up against the bed. His breathing turns labored.

"You best be going soon, so call your friends. I have some business to take care of," says Papa.

"I won't let you die alone," Marina declares. "We can wait on the far side if you need privacy for your business first."

"No, I suppose you should hear this as it concerns you." With effort, her father unfurls the blank scroll Mika had left on the end table and begins dictating to it.

The words appear as they leave his lips.

"I, Antonio Julius Castaloni, do hereby make the following adjustments to my last will and testament. Upon my passing, my sons, Gabriel and Jackson, and my wife, Corabelle, shall receive annual provisions equal to three times their current allotments.

"All lands and businesses connected to the Castaloni name shall pass to caretakers, should my heir choose not to run them herself. Such will be the case until a future grandchild or other descendant comes forth to claim their birthright. Furthermore, accounts shall be established for my daughter, Marina, in each of the neutral cities of Temperance, Outreach, and New Hope. Ten percent of the profits shall flow into these accounts as befits the rights of the firstborn. She and her descendants may draw upon these accounts at any point and use the funds as they wish, especially to facilitate closer ties among Arkonai and Saroth or to benefit causes that would aid the Bereft.

"I make these changes of my own free will. May the One be glorified in my life and through my death."

Marina's father slides his thumb down the side of the enchanted scroll until a single drop of blood forms. Letting the scroll curl back up, he seals it with this drop of blood.

Moved by his thoughtfulness in providing for her, Marina hugs her father tightly.

Chapter 23:
Vision Cast

Antonio's Private Chambers, Castaloni Estate, City of Outreach

"Call your other friends, Mari," says Marina's father, repeating an earlier sentiment. He's still holding her. "Mika's patience will not last much longer, and I think it best you leave before he returns."

Breaking out of the embrace, Marina nods.

"I can do that," Daniel assures them. Stepping off to the side, he quiets his mind and silently calls to Gabriella Ricci and Marcus Polani.

Soon, they use a Teleportation scroll to enter the room directly.

After exchanging pleasantries with Marina's father, Gabriella and Marcus look to Daniel.

"What do you require of us, Seeker?" asks Marcus, keeping his tone stiffly formal.

"With Master Antonio's permission, I will soon begin sifting through the room's past," Daniel explains. "I'll keep my focus on meals and drinks brought into the room as they're the most likely source for poison. I will need both of you to reach into my mind and transfer the images to Marina and her father."

"Sounds like a Vision Cast would be more effective," Gabriella comments. "That way we can see what you do as you come across the images."

Daniel shoots her a puzzled look.

"I've never heard of such a thing," he says. "How does it work?"

"Marcus can explain better than I can," says Gabriella. "I can't even do it with any consistency, but I can provide him with the extra mental support he'll likely need."

"I'll need focusing crystals or a large mirror," Marcus says.

"There are no focusing crystals, but you'll find a large mirror in the dressing room." Marina's father points to a curtain on the right side of the room as one enters.

Together, Daniel and Marcus wheel out an impressive mirror. The reflective area is wider across than Daniel can spread his arms. The height goes well above his head. They position the mirror at the foot of the bed, so Marina and her father can see it well.

Marcus frowns and looks uncomfortable.

"He needs to sit down for this," Gabriella explains. "Vision Casting is physically and mentally taxing work."

"May I?" Marcus waves to a spot at the end of the bed.

"Please. Do whatever you need to do with haste. My counselor will return shortly," says Marina's father.

"Where do you need me?" Daniel inquires.

"It doesn't really matter," Marcus answers, "but you might find a better flow of information from the room's center."

"Mari, come sit beside me," says her father.

By the time Daniel reaches the room's center, everyone else has found a good position. Marina now sits up near the headboard to her father's left. Marcus perches on the end a little to Marina's left. Gabriella sits directly behind him with her hands on his shoulders.

"We're ready," Gabriella announces.

Closing his eyes, Daniel stretches out with his Seeker Gifts.

The room brightens around him within his mind's eye. A soft gasp from Marina tells him something must be happening, but his position behind the mirror prevents him from seeing what Marcus is showing them.

Drawing deep, even breaths, Daniel scrolls back in time. First, he sees Marina speaking with her father before he arrived in the room. Next, he watches a series of people come and go. He slows the flow of images as meals are delivered and speeds up between visitors.

On separate occasions, Jackson, Gabriel, and a woman Daniel assumes is Corabelle Castaloni spend time with Marina's father. Servants come and go, seeing to the man's needs. Daniel pays more attention each time anybody delivers food or drinks to the room.

Dozens of deliveries happen without incident, but finally, an image flashes brighter in Daniel's mind, prompting him to pay attention. Backing up the image to review it, he lets it progress at normal speed. A male servant enters with a pot of tea. Marina's father occupies the bed sound asleep. After checking to confirm the condition of sleep, the servant slips something into the teapot.

The whole scene takes about eight seconds to complete.

Now that he has seen the servant's face, Daniel quickly moves to several other visits from the man. Twice more, Daniel sees the servant slip something into the tea.

Skipping back to a scene with Jackson, Daniel checks to see if the man consumes anything in the room. He does not. A check of several visits from Gabriel and Marina's mother show them often drinking or eating with her father, but each time, the tea or meal gets delivered by a female servant.

Letting the magic slip from his grasp, Daniel returns his attention to the present moment.

"Did it work?" he wonders. He can guess from their expressions that it has.

Marina appears agitated. Leaving her father's side, she paces on the far side of the bed.

Her father looks stricken.

"I will have to deal with this quietly," he murmurs.

"It's not enough," says Marina fiercely. "Gabriella, can you find the servant. His name is Tariel Marlo. I must know who put him up to this. He's been with this house forever."

Daniel moves to Marina's side in case she finds a use for him. The new position allows him to watch as a confusing mixture of images flash across the mirror. Jackson's face appears more than once, but the pictures change too rapidly for Daniel to make out anything.

They end abruptly as Marcus loses consciousness, leaning heavily back upon Gabriella.

She grunts and struggles to hold him up.

Rushing forward, Daniel catches hold of Marcus's shoulders long enough for Gabriella to scoot backwards far enough for him to be placed on the bed.

"Is he—" Daniel begins.

"He'll be fine in a minute," Gabriella says quickly. Her skin appears paler than normal.

"What did we just witness?" Marina asks.

Gabriella doesn't answer right away.

"I suspect already," says Marina, "but I need to know for sure."

"Your brother, Jackson, arranged for the poison through a series of threats against the servant's family," she explains. Twisting her head around, Gabriella casts a sympathetic glance at Marina's father. "I'm so sorry."

Marina and her father look stricken.

Daniel longs to comfort her but understands that she currently needs to share the moment of grief with her father.

As he draws this conclusion, Marina climbs back onto the bed and crawls over to her father.

They weep together.

Eventually, her father calls her name softly until he has her attention.

"Mari, you must go soon, but promise me two things. When I am gone, get Tariel and his family far out of Jackson's reach, and reconcile with your mother."

Marina pulls away to meet her father's eyes.

"Marcus and I can help with the servant and his family," Gabriella offers.

Marina smiles at her gratefully, but it fades when she turns to her father again.

"I will try."

Her father's gaze hardens.

"You will do better than try," he says. "Promise me."

"I—" Marina cuts herself off and bows her head. "Yes, Papa."

"Good girl. Now, be off. I must rest."

"I don't want to leave you," Marina whispers, clinging to her father's arms.

Pulling her forward, her father places a gentle kiss on her forehead.

"I wish you could stay too, but I'm afraid the guards would object to your company." Marina's father flicks his attention over to Daniel briefly.

Sensing the charge in the older man's eyes, Daniel nods solemnly.

"I am tired, my love," says her father, "and I have a lot of details to sort with Mika and your mother. Remember to tell the others what we discussed before. It will be hard, but you must keep your word. Trust in the One for guidance and peace and always remember how much I love you."

After one more, fierce hug, Marina climbs off the bed.

By this time, Gabriella has managed to awaken Marcus.

"We will meet you at the Temple as agreed," says Gabriella.

"He'll need some time to recover, but we'll make it."

Holding tight to Marcus, Gabriella reads from a Teleportation scroll.

Daniel doesn't know where it's set to, but he waves farewell anyway.

"Marina, we should leave as well," Daniel says, drawing out the last of the Teleportation scrolls Gabriel delivered upon their last meeting.

Daniel holds out his arms, and Marina walks willingly into his embrace. Once her arms tighten around him, Daniel begins reading silently.

The spell whisks them away from the Castaloni estate and places them in a quiet field on the edge of the Tranquil Plains, near the path up to the Alamon Temple. The protection wards surrounding the place prevent them from teleporting any closer.

The sudden isolation suits their mood well. Daniel maintains his hold on Marina until she pulls away. They share a long, sad look.

Gently, he takes her good hand and begins the long trek up to the Temple. At this pace, it might take them hours, but Daniel decides not to rush Marina. She needs the processing time. He lost his parents many years ago, but their deaths came suddenly. He didn't have to watch them waste away under a poison arranged for by a loved one. At various times throughout his life, Daniel has wished he had a sibling or two, but this is the first moment he gives silent thanks for having none to break his heart.

Chapter 24:
The Long Game

Jackson's Office, Fort Medron

Upon appearing back in his Fort Medron office, Jackson Castaloni immediately lights a fire in the hearth. He does so by conjuring a small fireball and hurling it at the wood carefully stacked for that purpose. Not satisfied, he tosses a few more pre-cut logs into place until the fire doubles then triples in size. Most people would back away from such intense heat, but Jackson relishes the warmth.

Do not despair. Things can still be made right.

"How?" Jackson demands. Disgust surrounds the word. "My father will die any day now, and the plan to sacrifice Marina to spark a war has utterly failed."

It was a good plan. Unfortunately, people are not as predictable as we would like them to be. Shall I move some other servants to deal with Lady Christa Arrington?

"No," Jackson answers immediately.

That is my point exactly.

"I don't understand, Master," Jackson admits.

You have never so much as met this Arkonai woman, yet you have already rendered a judgment on her behalf. Why would you do such a thing?

"I am not sure," Jackson says, searching his heart for an answer. "She showed good courage."

She refused to kill the architect of her misery. That is a foolish notion of mercy put there by the One.

"She is pleasing to the eye," Jackson adds.

Would you like her as a reward someday?

"No!" This denial carries more conviction. "She is Arkonai. I refuse to risk creating a half-breed."

That won't be a problem.

"What do you mean?" Jackson glares into the flames, since his master lacks a form to focus his anger upon.

Powerful magic always carries a price. To preserve your strength and youth, your body has naturally drawn power from other sources. You will never be a father in the physical sense. I intend to make you so much more. Family ties would only weaken you.

"How can I inherit if I cannot continue the Castaloni line? The house council will pass me over for Gabriel." Jackson can only clench and unclench his hands, trying to master his emotions.

Wait for your brother and his dear Tielle to have a child, and then remove them

The answer's simplicity surprises and unsettles Jackson. He sits down beside the fire to think. Gabriel has proven an inconsistent source of information at best, but Jackson cannot bring himself to condemn him completely.

During childhood, Jackson and Marina had competed for Gabriel's affections. She and their little brother had spent much time chasing each other around the woods behind one of the country estates near Jorash. Jackson recalls the countless hours he spent conjuring various objects for their amusement.

Now, he's orchestrating both of their downfalls.

"Is there no other way?" he wonders.

Not unless you can abide a child born of Marina and the huntsman.

The thought causes a visceral feeling of repulsion in Jackson.

I thought not, but do not worry about such matters now. We have more pressing concerns. You must continue your training in earnest and embark upon a new endeavor to kill your sister.

"Do I have your permission to act against her directly?" Jackson inquires.

Yes, but you must be careful. Nothing can point to you. If there's an opportunity to publicly reconcile with her, do so.

A sneer curls the corners of Jackson's lips. His fingers heat up as he remembers burning her request for a truce.

"What made you change your mind concerning her?" Jackson

wonders. It had surprised him when the Dark Man first approached him with the scheme that would have led to Marina being executed for the Supreme Huntmaster's assassination.

We may yet be able to use her death to increase tension between the magic races, but I now think it more likely her ideas of unity will infect the communities she encounters. It is vital that she not live long enough to foster a lasting peace.

"Where can I find her?" asks Jackson.

She is at the Alamon Temple making her union with the huntsman official, but that is far too public a place to deal with her. This may require some patience. They will likely settle in a neutral city at first, but eventually, they will find cities in general ill-suited to their needs.

"Should I prepare servants to act as spies?" asks Jackson. He doesn't bother questioning his master's powers of prediction. They have proven accurate in the past.

Marina has little use for servants, but that may be wise concerning your temporary sister, Gabriella.

"What about her?" In truth, Jackson had completely forgotten that scheme to officially unite the Castaloni and Polani houses by temporarily adopting Gabriella Ricci until her marriage to Marcus.

It is always good to have eyes and ears in powerful places. The Castaloni holdings will likely lavish gifts upon Gabriella and her husband-to-be. If you take an active hand in transferring personnel, you can find willing informants.

"How long will I have to pay them?" Jackson inquires.

As long as necessary. You can afford it. In the long game, it costs little to maintain opens lines of communication. Marcus is young now, but his Minder skills are formidable. That will attract attention in Dominance. Gabriella is less trained, but also powerful. Watch them closely. They could be useful or dangerous.

"Should I also take an active hand in making cities distasteful to Marina and the huntsman?" asks Jackson.

You won't have to. Natural prejudices and hatred will drive them away from heavily populated places soon enough. Even the neutral cities have plenty of problems. Besides, the huntsman will eventually return to his duties. That will likely keep them on the move.

An image of Christa Arrington dropping the dagger comes to mind. As much as Jackson has dreamed of ending Marina, he's never considered doing the deed himself. He honestly doesn't know if he can. It's one matter to order a person's death, and another issue altogether to wield the blade. He'd tried during the River's Edge affair, but that had been an impulsive move, nothing he had painstakingly planned for.

You will find a fitting end for her when the time comes. Perhaps by then you can summon a warrior from the Darklands to do your bidding. My servants from this side of the Veil will have to enter Aeris in greater numbers in the coming days. If you help me, I will make you king over this world.

"Thank you, Master." The response comes automatically, but Jackson is not sure what to think about such a lofty promise. His goal of controlling the lands and businesses bearing his family name seems petty by comparison.

What will I do with that much power?

A sense of the Dark Man's amusement sweeps over Jackson.

Anything you desire.

Chapter 25:
A Rare Occurrence

Keris Council's Private Meeting Chamber, Alamon Temple
The dark green dress feels strange and wonderful to Marina after so many months wearing simple travel robes. She fully expected to exchange vows with Daniel in the clothes she wore walking out of Aridel's Northgate Prison, but her brother and friends had other plans. Gabriel met them at the Alamon Temple's gate with Tielle, a pair of servants, and a trunk of clothes.

After a happy reunion with Gabriel, Tielle, Greta, and Ciara, Marina let the women sweep her up to a private chamber already prepared for her. Over the next few hours, they had fussed over Marina, helping her wash away the remaining prison dust. Then, Greta helped her choose among the four dresses brought for the occasion, hand-picked by Marina's mother, while Ciara braided, folded, and pinned her hair into place.

Marina would trade every dress she ever owned for her mother's presence, but she understands the difficult position she's placed her family in. Regardless of her father's sympathy, the official house stance must stay neutral. Prejudices run too deep for them to openly embrace her radical choice to marry an Arkonai man. Besides, she cannot begrudge her mother's desire to spend every last second she can with her father.

"This is a rare occurrence indeed."

Huntmaster Taron's comment pulls Marina away from her thoughts.

"Before we get to the official ceremony, you must answer a few questions to our satisfaction." The huntmaster waves to his colleague.

The older woman wears flowing light brown robes like the huntmaster. Her only adornment, a bright red Keeper's pendant, hangs over her heart. It reminds Marina of the pendant Jack destroyed in the forest near River's Edge, but she pushes those painful memories away.

"We perform many mixed weddings between Bereft and Saroth or Bereft and Arkonai couples, but none between Arkonai and Saroth. Do you know why this is?" The lady stares at Daniel, awaiting his answer.

Daniel shoots a nervous glance at Marina.

"Something to do with a prophecy," he murmurs.

"And your answer?" Huntmaster Taron prompts Marina.

Having given the matter much thought over the past few months as she acknowledged her growing affection for Daniel, Marina has a ready answer.

"I believe it stems from a misunderstanding that the magic lines must be separate to stay pure," she says. "There is a prophecy that speaks of a child bearing mixed lineage changing the world, but the scholars are divided on how best to interpret such a prediction. They cannot even tell if the change is for the better."

"Do you fear this prophecy?" asks Huntmaster Taron.

"We choose not to fear what we do not understand," Daniel answers, speaking the conclusion they discussed together previously. He clasps his hands in front of his body to keep from reaching for Marina's hand before he's allowed to do so.

"Do you intend to have children?" This question comes from the Minder, Lady Gera.

Marina feels her cheeks flush.

"We've not really discussed the topic at length, but if the One and the Lady bless us with children, we will count it an honor to be entrusted with their care."

"How did you meet?" inquires Huntmaster Taron.

Daniel clears his throat nervously.

"I ... accepted a contract on Marina's life but realized her innocence and chose to break the contract."

"And the High Council simply accepted this?" asks Huntmaster Taron. His eyes twinkle with mirth, telling Marina he knows their response was not favorable.

"No, sir," says Daniel. "They did not."

"Yet you are here," concludes Huntmaster Taron. "Their full forgiveness may take time, but it will come. Have patience. It will take the Interim Supreme Huntmaster time to learn his way. Do you intend to continue your career as a huntsman?"

"If I may," Daniel answers. He casts a small smile at Marina. "And if my wife agrees that I should."

"Wise man," comments Huntmaster Taron. "We do not have time to hear the full tale here, though I would enjoy listening to the broader account later, but tell us, what brings you to seek a union at the Alamon Temple?"

"Circumstances brought me to the Northgate Prison in the city of Aridel," Marina explains. "The High Council wanted Daniel to question me. That made him a frequent visitor to my cell." She shifts her gaze from the huntmaster and the Minder over to Daniel. "I think it was over the course of those many conversations that our friendship deepened into more."

"I think I loved her when I laid eyes on her," says Daniel. "She was carrying a child, a boy stricken by Surdan's Bane. I'd never seen such a combination of fierce determination and endless compassion."

Lady Gera nods, accepting both answers before turning her attention to Marina.

"If your husband continues his work with the Arkonai Hunting Guild, he may be away for long periods of time, what will you do without him?"

"I would like to continue my studies to bring people relief from pain and help my friend continue using his Destroyer Gifts to heal diseases."

"There's great sadness in you," notes Lady Gera. "You once possessed Destroyer Gifts."

It's not a question, but Marina elaborates anyway.

"The One has seen fit to change the course of my life," she begins. "I wish I could graciously accept this, but I miss the familiarity of my Destroyer Gifts, even though I chose not to employ them traditionally."

"You have always desired to be a healer but believed it not in your true gifting," says Lady Gera. "But possessing Healer Gifts has little to do with being one. That is a heart matter, and I believe you possess such a heart. You are a healer, Marina Castaloni."

Marina lets her eyes shut while she absorbs the Minder's words. She smiles her thanks but doesn't try to speak for fear she'll start crying.

"Speaking your name reminds me. Naming customs for united couples differ for Arkonai and Saroth. If you follow Arkonai tradition, you should take your husband's surname as your own. If you keep to Saroth custom, the Castaloni name would prevail due to house rank. Have you considered this?" asks Lady Gera.

"I have," Marina answers. "And we did discuss names at length."
That might have qualified as our first argument.

A faint smile from Lady Gera tells Marina she broadcast the thought.

"What is your decision?" inquires Huntmaster Taron, recapturing her attention.

"Daniel will change nothing about his name, but I will join our two surnames," Marina announces. "I am equally proud to continue wearing the Castaloni name as I am to join with my husband and accept his name as part of who I am."

Huntmaster Taron rubs his chin thoughtfully.

"It's not done often, but aye, that is an acceptable solution," says Huntmaster Taron. "I assume you agreed to this?" He points the question at Daniel with his eyes.

"I wasn't happy at first," Daniel admits, "but it is an acceptable compromise."

The huntmaster and the Minder exchange a significant look.

"We are satisfied with your answers," reports the huntmaster.

"Please introduce us to your guests, and we will begin the ceremony," says Lady Gera.

In addition to the small party that came with Gabriel, Marina introduces Marcus Polari, Gabriella Castaloni, Kyle Ricci, and Daria Toscano, sent on behalf of Marina's mother. She almost called Gabriella by her old name, but the ceremonial adoption was finalized by the Tariku League a few days ago. Marina makes the introductions even though Gabriella and Kyle are known to Lady Gera since the former spent some time studying with her.

Next, Daniel presents Annie Kerns, sent on behalf of Lady Christa Arrington. Unfortunately, handling her uncle's affairs and helping her intended settle into his new role prevents Christa from attending personally. Jordan Lekros too has his Supreme Huntmaster training to attend to instead of bearing witness to their ceremony.

The scene doesn't match the image Marina conjured in her head as a child when picturing her wedding, but peace and contentment surround her anyway. Sorrow tries to intrude, reminding her that neither of their parents could attend, but she pushes it away with effort.

"Thank you, one and all, for coming to witness the union of

these two souls," says Lady Gera. "Your presence reminds us that life is better when spent with family and friends."

"Did you prepare vows, or would you like us to select some for you?" inquires Huntmaster Taron.

"We have chosen to speak for ourselves," Daniel answers.

"I thought that might be the case," says Lady Gera. She waves for them to kneel on the thin white cushions placed between them. "Please face each other and clasp hands, palms facing forward toward each other."

Marina holds out both hands.

Daniel aligns his palms to hers and folds his fingers through hers.

"It's customary to give short opening speeches before voicing any vows. Who would like to speak first?" asks Huntmaster Taron.

"He can," says Marina.

"Marina," says Daniel at the same moment.

They laugh nervously.

He squeezes her hands gently to encourage her to speak.

"Daniel Saveron, the world says we should be enemies," Marina begins. She shakes her head. "But I don't believe that. I want to know you more. I want to see the world through your eyes. With an open mind and an open heart we could change everything. There's so much I can learn from you. There's so much I could teach you. Do you believe in us? Do you believe we could change everything?"

"I believe in us," Daniel answers softly. "You have already changed me. I believe the One has made you for me and me for you. We have knelt alone, but we will rise together, united in heart and soul."

"Your friends and family have gathered to bear witness to sacred promises you make to each other before the One this day," says Lady Gera. "You have chosen to speak from the heart, but before you do so, I will ask you to change the position of your hands."

She motions for them to break contact, so they untwine their fingers and pull their hands back.

"Daniel, please reach out with your right hand and grasp Marina's right wrist," Minder Gera instructs. "Marina, do the same with Daniel's left wrist."

Typically, the hands would be clasped in a crossed manner, but Lady Gera must have adapted the ceremony to accommodate Marina's damaged right hand. Healing is happening at a much slower pace than anticipated.

Once their hands are situated, the Minder nods at Marina to

speak first.

"Daniel Saveron, from this day forward I will gladly call you my husband. I will go where you go, work with you to create a home, and stand by you in trouble and in peace. Your causes will be my causes, your pains will become mine, and your victories too will be mine."

"Marina Castaloni, from this day forward I will gladly call you my wife. Your causes will be mine. I will seek to protect you, to provide for you, and to comfort you for the rest of my days. All that is mine will be yours, as I am yours completely."

"Well said," comments Huntmaster Taron.

He places his right hand on Daniel's shoulder and his left hand on Marina's shoulder.

Lady Gera ducks under his arms and leans over them, placing her hands atop theirs.

"May what the One has bound together last forever," she says.

"You may rise as husband and wife," adds Huntmaster Taron.

Lady Gera pulls her hands away from them.

Daniel propels himself to his feet and pulls Marina up with him. His arms settle around her waist, while hers loop around his neck. With a smooth, twisting motion, Daniel lifts her over the cushions and sets her on her feet with her back to their guests. Joy lights up his countenance, but Marina doesn't see the expression long.

Closing her eyes, she rises up on her tiptoes to meet his kiss.

For a magical moment, Marina forgets anybody else exists, but eventually, the kiss ends, and she opens her eyes to the new reality.

She has a husband. She has a future to build with him.

They will spend the next few days planning at the Temple, but beyond that, Marina has no idea where they will go. Quite a few places ought to be avoided because they possess large numbers of fanatical Arkonai or Saroth, but it's a big world with plenty of free land. The freedom and uncertainty exhilarate and terrify her.

Do not worry about tomorrow, dear one. Tomorrow will come in its own time. Enjoy the peace of this moment.

Accepting the One's advice, Marina pulls her new husband along to greet their guests.

Soon, she's lifted off her feet again, this time by her tall baby brother.

"Congratulations!" Gabriel shouts. Lowering his voice to a whisper, he continues, "I'm glad I chose you."

Marina returns her brother's enthusiastic hug, but his words disquiet her heart. Once Jackson knows of Gabriel's support, he will not be pleased.

"I'm glad you came," says Marina, releasing her hold on him.

Tielle immediately takes Gabriel's place.

"That was beautiful!" She steps back, takes hold of Gabriel's left arm, and smiles shyly. "We'll have to ask you to help us write our vows someday."

"I don't remember a word I said," says Daniel. "I was so nervous."

Hearing his comment, Lady Gera chuckles.

"I remember them," she says, "and I will have them recorded for you before you leave if you like."

"That would be nice," says Marina. "We would like that very much." Thinking it might be a lot of work, she adds, "But please don't go out of your way for us."

"Let me give you this small gift," says the Minder. "It will give me something to do this evening."

They graciously accept, and the Minder steps away so more guests can approach them.

"I also have a gift for you," Gabriella announces, "but it will take some explaining. Seek me out later when you can get away." She nods toward a back corner where Marcus Polani retreated to stay out of the way. "We're going for a walk in the gardens. You can find us there for the next few hours or have Daria Toscano find us later, but don't worry if you miss us. We're not leaving until tomorrow afternoon." She then throws her arms around both of their waists and draws them into a tight hug. "Marcus isn't the hug-in-public type," Gabriella says, once she finally lets go. "But he's thrilled for you too." With that, she leaves before Marina or Daniel can even think of a proper response.

"She would definitely be a squirrel if she was a Shapeshifter," Gabriel comments, watching his friend's bouncing retreat.

Daniel gives Gabriel a strange look that makes Marina laugh.

It's going to be an interesting life with you, Daniel Saveron.

Epilogue:
Keeper of the Will

Corabelle's Office, Castaloni Estate, City of Outreach

The door to Corabelle Castaloni's office swings open slowly, admitting Mika Forester. The man's posture remains stiff until the door clicks shut behind him. When they're alone, his expression changes from neutral to something more suited to a man who recently lost a dear friend.

He knew Antonio longer than I did.

The realization brings Corabelle up out of her seat, but she resists the urge to cross over to him. She fears offering any emotional support will collapse her own. If she had her way, the coming conversation would wait until after a proper mourning period.

But waiting could get somebody killed, so it's not an option.

"I am so sorry for your loss," Mika says quietly.

Corabelle acknowledges his sympathy with a nod and bids him to take a seat with a wave.

They each collapse into a chair.

She needs a moment to regain the little emotional margin she had scraped together to hold this meeting with the counselor and purser. Having both jobs attended to by the same man is highly unusual and clearly demonstrated Antonio's unwavering trust in his childhood friend. Over the years, Corabelle has worked very hard to keep Mika on her side.

"Have you had a chance to read the will with the recent amendments, my lady?" asks Mika.

"It doesn't surprise me," Corabelle remarks by way of answering. She has thought of little else since her husband's death two days prior.

The entire future of the house rests upon her. Antonio's provisions for Marina will be heavily contested but likely stand if she supports them. If she opposes them, the house council will elect a new heir or split the properties evenly between her sons.

"What would you like me to do about it?" Mika prompts. "I have filed the amendments, but they are still within my reach if you want them retrieved."

"What do you think I should do?" Corabelle wonders.

Mika's lips form a thin line as he holds in a response.

"I have an answer," Corabelle assures the man, "but I still value your advice." When he again says nothing, she continues, "You may speak freely without fear of raising my anger. I know my children and their faults well enough by now. I have put a privacy spell in place already, but you may also add one if that makes you feel more comfortable." She gestures to the spent scroll sitting in the center of her desk.

"Whether you leave things as Antonio wishes or not, Jackson will sue for control of everything," says Mika. "He's not the best candidate, but the house council will likely confirm him as the true heir if you let the original document stand without the amendment. The new document gives you more options, but he may yet prevail. He's very, ambitious." Mika's eyes flash with warning.

"You can say it," Corabelle says softly. "I can't bring myself to, but I am not blind."

Only heartbroken.

"We both know Antonio's illness had mysterious origins." Despite the privacy spell, Mika drops his voice level. "There's no proof, and I think seeking proof would only lead to disaster as that would certainly fall under the Unforgivable Crimes Act. I do not envy the decision that lies before you. Letting Jackson inherit will impact business negatively, but it's also the safest option for many people, including you and your other children ... unless you give me leave to take appropriate measures."

Corabelle winces at his last words. She had braced herself for them, but still feels pain blossom in the center of her chest. An image of Jackson as a toddler comes to mind. His Conjurer Gifts had manifested before he could even walk. They had felt something strange from his nursery late one night, rushed in, and found him surrounded by stuffed animals with Marina standing near the crib. Antonio had chided Marina for moving the toys, but Corabelle had known better. Jackson had been instinctively conjuring the items into his crib.

"I will not order my son's death." Corabelle shakes off both mental images.

"Even if it might spare the other two?" Mika's eyes radiate compassion.

Setting both hands on her desk, Corabelle curls them into fists so tight she risks drawing blood. She suddenly wishes she had the faith of her late husband and her firstborn. She could certainly use a measure of peace.

"I am trying desperately not to destroy my family." Corabelle lowers her head into her hands to gather her scattered wits.

"Will you support Jackson then?" Mika's tone tries for neutral but still carries disapproval.

Lifting her head out of her hands, Corabelle sits up straighter, working hard to compose herself.

"No, but I think it best we let him think I do," she says.

Mika looks intrigued by her statement.

"How can we do that?" he wonders.

"File Antonio's amendment securing Marina's position yet allowing her to choose her own path," Corabelle instructs the counselor. "Allow Jackson the illusion that he might inherit if he meets certain goals. Increase his allowance so that it's close to what he would receive if he had inherited outright. Use part of my share and Gabriel's if you must."

"Do you believe the extra money will sate his ambitions?" asks Mika.

"Not really, but make sure it's clear that certain responsibilities come with the prospects and he may lose interest and settle for a lesser annual sum in exchange for relief from those responsibilities," she explains.

Mika smiles for the first time.

"Shall I add some responsibilities even if there are none, Lady Corabelle?"

"Please do," she says. "My hope is that Jackson will entrust most of the daily oversight responsibilities to Gabriel. Move Gabriel and his intended to whichever estate is farthest from Jackson's current residence."

"He's a Master Conjurer," Mika points out. "He could be there in an instant."

"Keep them moving if you have to," instructs Corabelle. "If they will stand for it, hire guards for them as they tour the various facilities. Tielle has some skill in the Conjuring arts. Find a job for her to do that keeps her surrounded by people every moment she's out of Gabriel's sight."

"That should keep them safe," Mika says, looking cautiously hopeful. "What of Marina? I can hold Jackson's claim at bay a few years with no problem, up to ten if he knows little of the mechanics of the house council, but his only clear path to the whole is through her and her family, now that she has a husband."

A pang runs through Corabelle at missing the key moment in her daughter's life, but if she wants to ensure Marina has a future, sacrifices must be made.

"I have made some arrangements for her through Gabriella," says Corabelle.

"The Minder adopted to unite the house with the Polani family?" Mika's muttered question is half-statement and half-inquiry. "What can she do?"

"She assures me it's possible to shield Marina and Daniel from Arkonai Seekers and other Minders," Corabelle explains. "I have asked her to do this for them, though she refused any sort of payment. She is also suppressing Gabriel's knowledge that Antonio is gone to keep Marina away from the funeral for her sake. In a few days, I will explain my actions to Marina at the Alamon Temple or wherever she is at that point." She swallows hard. "She may not forgive me. That may be the last time I see her in this life, but if it keeps her alive, so be it."

A fresh ache blasts through Corabelle, making breathing difficult. She has gone these past few years without laying eyes upon her daughter, but that was Marina's choice and a different matter entirely. The prospect of needing to be seen cutting ties with her hurts deeply.

Mika lets several beats pass before raising a new delicate matter.

"What public stance will you take in these matters, my lady?" asks the counselor. "Officially, you are the public voice for the house council. Everyone will wish to know where you stand."

"Neutral," Corabelle says, absolutely meaning it. "I have no desire to see these matters tear all remaining bonds that exist between my children, but I also will not risk the utter chaos an open contest among them would cause the businesses and lands. People depend on us."

"Privately supporting Marina while publicly remaining neutral will disappoint the masses and frustrate Jackson," Mika warns.

"Do what you can to convince him I'm on his side," says Corabelle, "but I do not fear for my life. He doesn't believe I hold any power over him, and officially, that is the way of things. And continue to keep close confidence with him. He must not suspect anything."

"Shall I hire guards for you as well?" asks Mika.

Corabelle shakes her head.

"That won't be necessary. I will be assuming an honorary, non-voting position on the Tariku League soon," says Corabelle. "It's part of the arrangement Marcus Polani and I came to when he broke the first marriage contract with us."

"I had forgotten about that provision." Relief washes over Mika's face.

"I believe Jackson can be saved from himself," Corabelle says. "He only needs to find his way." The assurance fails to settle anything within her.

"I hope you're right, my lady." Mika struggles to a standing position and holds his hand out toward Corabelle.

She rises and briefly grasps his hand.

The counselor bows over her hand before releasing it.

"I will see you for the funeral tomorrow," says Mika. "Meanwhile, I shall arrange for the reading of the will and set the other things we discussed in motion. May the One have mercy on this house."

As soon as the door shuts behind the counselor, Corabelle sinks onto her chair and lets down her emotional guards. Tears fall suddenly in great streams. She weeps for her dead husband, her broken family, and the innocent people who will inevitably get caught up in the conflict if her plan to mollify Jackson fails.

An image of Antonio comes to her clearly, smiling that irresistible grin she fell in love with a lifetime ago.

Love them all.

Corabelle can't be certain if the thought comes from her or her late husband, but she accepts them at face value.

I will try, Antonio. I will try. They are all I have left of you.

THE END

Thank You for Reading:

Whether this is your first adventure in Aeris or simply the latest, I hope you enjoyed hearing some of Marina and Daniel's tale. There's certainly more to come for them in *The Dark Man's Wrath* and *The Lady's Grace*. If you want to skip their adventures and move directly into Redeemer Chronicles, that's also an option. As always, if you enjoyed the story, reviews are much appreciated.

Aeris stories in order: *River's Edge Ransom*, *The Huntsman and the Healer*, *The Dark Man's Wrath*, *The Lady's Grace*, *Awakening*, *The Holy War*, and *Reclaim the Darklands*.

Please visit my website: **www.juliecgilbert.com**. Check out the audiobooks. They have fantastic narrators. Or try a paperback.

I would love to connect via email:
devyaschildren@gmail.com

Other Contacts:
www.facebook.com/JulieCGilbert2013
www.instagram.com/juliecgilbert_writer/
https://twitter.com/authorgilbert
www.bookbub.com/authors/julie-c-gilbert